POSTHUMOUS PAPERS

OF THE

CADGERS' CLUB,

CONTAINING THE

LIVES, CHARACTERS, AND INTERESTING ANECDOTES,

OF THE

MEMBERS OF THAT CELEBRATED BODY.

———

𝕎ith 𝔈ighteen 𝔖uperior 𝔈ngrabings.

———

LONDON:

PUBLISHED BY E. LLOYD, BROAD-STREET, BLOOMSBURY.

1838.

ADDRESS.

———⋙✠⋘———

WE are unfortunately compelled, owing to the sudden dissolution of the august *Society of Cadgers,* and the stoppage of their private documents, to conclude this extraordinary work rather abruptly; this is the more vexatious, as the work has been a source of immense profit to us, as well as interest to the public—if we may be allowed to judge of their admiration, by the patronage they have bestowed upon us.

The editor of these *chronicles* regrets that he cannot at present publish any more of the curious proceedings and tales of that society; but should an opportunity present itself of his once more getting possession of the invaluable papers, the public may rest assured that they shall be presented to them in print immediately, by

Their humble Servant,

The EDITOR.

March 22, 1838.

POSTHUMOUS PAPERS

OF THE

CADGERS' CLUB.

CJG

CHAPTER I.

THE READER IS INTRODUCED TO THE GRAND SOCIETY OF METROPOLITAN STREET CADGERS.—A VIVID DESCRIPTION OF THE "CADGERS' SNUGERY."—ANECDOTES, ECCENTRICITIES, AND REVELRY OF THE MEMBERS.—SOME OF THE SECRETS OF TRADE DEVELOPED, AND INNUMERABLE OTHER FACTS, WHICH WILL BE FOUND AS INTERESTING AS THEY ARE IMPORTANT.—THE CADGERS' SUPPER, AND THE CADGERS' BALL.

UPON the commencement of a work which will involve the tremendous interest of the present remarkable narrative—an interest which will even eclipse, it is expected, the most distinguished history of the transactions of "The Pickwick Club"—it may probably be considered necessary to make the reader acquainted with a brief history of the Editor, and to give a summary of those unprecedented qualifications which obtained for him the great honour of transmitting these illustrious memorials to posterity. This we shall perform in as few words as possible, simply for two reasons—the first of which is, that our inherent modesty renders it an unpleasant task to talk of ourselves; and the second, because we are anxious to gratify our readers as soon as possible, with the life, fun, frolic, and facetiæ, we have in store for them.

Be it known, then, that the Editor of the "*Posthumous Papers of the Cadgers' Club,*" is 'an old one upon the town,' up to every move, down to every dodge, *wideo* upon every thing, and awake at all times; a gentleman by birth, a rogue by profession—being one of the principal M. C. C.'s, and clerk in ordinary to the "United Metropolitan Street Tradesmen!"

It is now ten years ago, since the society, whose secret transactions we are about to record, first shed the glorious effulgence of its light and wisdom upon the *lower* world. The magnanimous, all-learned, and indefatigable Mr. Pickwick, had already opened the channels of enterprise and learning, by founding his immortal Club, and himself and his renowned colleagues were busily engaged in spreading awide that universal spirit of adventure and philosophical discovery, which has since so greatly contributed to the enlightenment and the delight of mankind; the public seized upon the glorious idea with avidity, and it was truly remarkable to see the extraordinary effect it had upon all classes of society; clubs sprung up in every direction; the dustmen formed themselves into a society, the principal object of which was, to mature their knowledge in the *belles lettres*; the chummies combined together, and exerted themselves most strenuously in the study of the *black* art, but this being rather too *high* for their comprehension, the chummies quickly went to *pot*, and their society was shortly *swept* away. The scavengers also united, but their proceedings turned out to be all *muck*, and in consequence they went where they ought to be consigned—to the *kennel*. After these signal failures, it was never anticipated that there would be any possibility of establishing any other society, which might justly compete with that of the noble Pickwickians, nor was the slightest idea entertained that there would ever be found in the world, a man who could possess the stupendous mind of the amiable founder of that celebrated club;—weak notion! ridiculous thought! Not many months were suffered to pass by, ere there was another luminary ordained to break forth in the hemisphere of sublunary wisdom; not many months elapsed ere there was a combination of magnificent orbs, of equal if not surpassing brilliancy, whose proceedings and transactions were of that deeply interesting and important description, that the public have been awaiting, with almost insupportable suspense and anxiety, the happy moment when we should be enabled to confer a lasting obligation upon them, by communicating the same to them.

But where did this immortal individual spring from? to whom is the world at large indebted for the formation of a club, which will be distinguished, in the annals of fun, life, and adventure, above all other combinations in the world? Did this resplendent luminary first burst forth in magnificent lustre, irradiating the aristocratic and fashionable part of the world? No; but in the dark and dismal purlieus of that romantic spot, so celebrated in history as having formed the principal resort and the place of nativity of some of the most renowned heroes whose names are so immortalized in the annals of the country, for their strenuous exertions in peopleing Botany Bay, yclept Saint Giles's.

Yes, it was there that the glorious club whose adventures will illumine the pages of this work, was first established; it was there that its most magnanimous, enterprising, and ever to be honoured founder, the great, the sagacious, the learned, and esteemed *cadger*, Jeremiah Jumper, first drew the breath of life; it was there in a four story back attic he vegetated, and it was there the splendid idea first occurred to him, of establishing a club of those worthy brothers of his profession, who had distinguished themselves by their industrious traffic upon the public gullibility, by any particular feats of sagacity in the intricate and clever art of cadging !—Amiable Jeremiah! his name deserves to be carved in letters of gold upon the hearts of every *professional* street tradesman;—his memory must live for ever!

Jeremiah Jumper was a great man with a little body; he was about three feet four without his wooden legs, of which he had two, with a hump upon his back like Æsop, and a face whose expression was most remarkably intellectual, even encrusted as it was constantly with the marks of his profession, he being a first rate crossing sweeper of some years standing, on one of the most lucrative beats in the west end of the town. His person was always gracefully attired in a coat of various colours, mud monopolizing the principal portion of it, a pair of ragged corderoys encased his stumps, and the remnant of a hat minus a crown and half the brim, usually surmounted his head; the learned gentleman discarded a shirt as a superfluous article of dress with any respectable cadger. Jeremiah had formerly made a considerable deal of ready by *gammoning* the old sailor, which he afterwards abandoned for the soldier, until having become stale in both these characters, he forsook them for the impressive impersonation in which we have introduced him to our readers. This then was the illustrious vagrant to whom the world is so largely indebted for the formation of the Cadgers' Club! From him originated those invaluable documents which we, as the clerk of the society, have been permitted to submit to the public.

The objects of the "Cadgers' Club," were to form a union of all those respectable individuals who obtained a living by duping the public, and those who were the most expert rogues were considered the most efficient members. None were admitted who had not distinguished themselves by some particular deed or adventure, and it was ordered that they nightly meet at " *the Cadgers' Snuggery*," to report proceedings, relate their adventures, propose new schemes, elect new members, carouse, and enjoy themselves!—No person was allowed to take up a crossing until he had been duly appointed by the society, and till his qualifications were known and approved. The club to be conducted by a president, vice president, and secretary, and to be supported by the weekly contributions of the members. All members who were in distress from a depression of *business* to be relieved from the funds of the society, which same funds were to be holden by the honourable secretary and founder Jeremiah Jumper, Esq. S. G. C. M. C. C. Ordered too, that branch lodges be held in various parts of the country, the corresponding members of which were to report all proceedings to the Grand Lodge, "The Cadgers' Snuggery," Back Slums, Saint Giles's.

No sooner was the joyful news spread afar, that this glorious society was in existence, than numbers flocked to the Grand Lodge to enroll their names amongst those of its august members !—Never was such deep interest excited !—The crossing clenser *brushed* from his cross;—the blind opened their eyes;—the lame took up their legs and walked, the Snuggery was nightly crowded;—and the name of the immortal founder was lauded in terms of unqualified admiration, veneration, and esteem !—Saint Giles's and its neighbourhood received unfading lustre from its being known to be the glorious spot from which sprung that unequalled society, whose proceedings were so soon to diffuse the light of universal knowledge among the whole of the cadging fraturnity !

We commence the history of the mighty proceedings of this august society, on the first quarterly meeting of the Members, at the Snuggery; Billy Bimper, *Mechanic out of work, gammoner* president, *Jack the Scraper*, who worked as a blind fiddler, vice chairman. The Members were all met, and the scene which now presented itself was one of the most intensely interesting that can be imagined; we, even *we*, who wield so powerful a pen, despair of being able to do ample justice to it !—The place in which this renowned society held its meetings, was a large wooden building at the back of a dirty public house in Bainbridge street, Saint Giles' !—It was very large, very dark, and very dirty; its roof and sides were blackened with the immense volumes of smoke which were puffed forth so profusely from the lips of the occupants, and it was dimly lighted by a tin lamp suspended from the centre of the roof. The walls were copiously decorated with elegant embellishments, and tasty designs in chalk, striking portraits of the members, more particularly a full length one of the mighty founder, which ornamented the further end of the room, immediately behind the president's chair. In addition to these ornaments, there were innumerable printed bills of last dying speeches, and other exquisite and rare *morceaus* of the like choice and invaluable description. Wooden legs, birch brooms, crutches, and other symbols of the professions of the members, which had either been discarded by them on their entering the room, or were ready for the use of any new elected member, whose inclination might tempt him to adopt any one of those innocent and honourable methods of getting a living. The entrance to this apartment was by means of a trap-door in the flooring, and no one was admitted until he had by giving the secret watchword of the society, convinced them that he was not a spy upon their proceedings; thus it will be seen that had not the task been deputed to one of its members, this unequalled history could never have been sent forth to delight the public. In the centre of the room was a long table with forms around it, and elevated seats at each end for the Chairman and Vice Chairman, and on those forms, and in those elevated seats, were seated the celebrated personages whose wonderful exploits will shine so brilliantly in these pages, with pint measures full of that very exhilarating beverage called "Cream of the Valley" before them, and letting the steam off at their heads, from pipes varying in length from a dudee to an alderman! There were sailors who had never seen the sea; soldiers who had never been in any regiment; fit shamers, timber merchants, *alias*, match venders; poor mechanics; reduced noblemen, knights of the broom, poor starving tradesmen, and every possible description of cadger to be met with in the great metropolis. At the head of the table was seated in all the dignity of a nabob, the redoutable president, Billy Bumper; his outward man attired in a dingy black coat, very much delapidated at the elbows and under the arms, underneath which was a ruinous waistcoat, and before him hung a white apron. He was a straight haired, small eyed, sleek faced, sagacious looking individual, and seemed to feel the dignity of, the highly responsible and important situation he had the honour to fill. In one hand he held a quart pot, with the delicious contents of which he had just been luxuriating his thorax, and in the other he clutched a broken crutch, with the head of which he occasionally hammered upon the table to enforce order and decorum. The Vice Chairman "*Jack the Scraper*," was a peculiarly interesting looking gentleman in ragged clothes, a ragged head of hair, and a countenance which had been beautifully macadamized by the small pox. He had for thirty years been collecting the tin by torturing the cat-gut, and gammoning blind.—He might truly be said to have made a fortune with his eyes shut. But if these two personages excited the interest and and attention of the numerous members of that illustrious Club, what was it compared to the profound esteem, the enthusiastic admiration; the unspeakable rapture with which they gazed upon the remarkable, and prepossessing figure of their distinguished founder, who, seated on the right hand of the chairman, with his arms folded, and his wooden supporters resting along the form, drew all hearts towards him, and cast a magnificence around him, almost too powerful for contemplation!—Yes, there, in that brief space, sat the indescribable, the incomparable rival of the all-powerful Mr. Pickwick!—the most stupendous Jeremiah Jumper. Nothing could equal the enthusiasm and veneration evinced by every person present, towards that celebrated man; glasses were handed, quart pots, brimfull of "Dog's Nose," were thrust upon him, out of each of which the good man kindly condescended to quaff a greater portion of the contents, to the infinite gratification of all present.

The members being all assembled, order was obtained, and the chairman arose to address the meeting. First he scratched his learned head, and then he gracefully spat forth a large quid of tobacco under the table, rinced his mouth with the half of a crown bowl of punch, and thus elegantly began :—

"Gemmen o' th' Cadgers' Club, it is vith feelin's o' werry great pleasure I rises to *undress* ye on this here occashun ; this here is the fust kevarterly meetin' o' this here werry 'spectable community, an' I feels remarkable proud to announce to yer as how ve gets on out an' out !—*(a simultaneous cry of " Good luck !")* Yes, gemmen, th' Cadgers' 'sciety is fast *transgressin'* ! *(Cheers.)* In these here three months ve has helected, no lesserer than tventy three 'spectable cross sveepers, ten timber marchants, three letter fakers, von Smith'eld ranter, an' thirteen vipe divers ! *(Boisterous cries of Bravo !)* It may p'rhaps be as vell jist to state here, in *delushun* to th' latter branch, that it is vith werry much regret, I has

to state there is a 'markable falling off in trade ; svells gets werry stingy, an' vill not sport their fogles as they used to do, an' it has been proved 'fra unkaveshtunable 'thority, as how those here as does sport 'em out at all, has 'em act'wully sewn to the bottom o' their pocket ! *(Loud groans and cries of " Shame !")*— Gemmen I am delighted to hinform yer, that th' mopusses has tumbled in in werry good style into our funds since th' 'stablishment on our Club, an' there is no doubt, as how in the course on a werry short time, ve may hold up our heads vith any on th' nobby 'scieties in the known vorld ! *(Tremendous shouts.)* It must be extremely gratifying to yer all to hear on th' falling off on th' success on th' Mendicity 'sciety ! *(Loud cries of Bravo ! intermixed with groans.)* That 'ere 'sciety ought to be despised by ev'ry 'spectable cadger ; vouldn't they feed us on skillee an' soup ? *(Shame ! shame.)* Havn't they th' audacity to tell us to vork, an' if ve don't ve are sent to grind vin' ? *(Groans and cries of shame !)* Yes, gemmen, it is a shame !—Vot right hav' ve to vork vhen there's so much ochre in th' vorld ? *(Hear ! hear!)* A'n't ve as good gemmen as any on 'em, ve is, and gemmen ve vill remain ! (*Cheers.*) I shall conclude this 'ere long patter, as I'm not much used to speechify, by proposing a toast in vhich I knows you vill all cordiwully join, " Success to the " *Cadgers' Club*," and long life an' success to it's larned founder Jeremiah Jumper, Eskever, S. G. C. &. M. C. C. !"

This eloquent and appropiate speech was received with the most deafening applause, but upon the proposition of the toast, a shout so boisterous, so simultaneous, so enthusiastic burst from every lip, that it made the beams of the apartment rattle, and resounded from one end of Saint Giles's to the other ; quart pots were hammered upon the table ; glasses jingled, crutches were flourished in the air, and wooden legs were thumped upon the floor, and every thing evinced the most lively interest imaginable !—A more glorious scene could not have been conceived ; the toast was drank with nine times nine ; how must the learned bosom of the distinguished muck-groveler have glowed at this small tribute to his immense worth and talent !—When the deafening shouts had gradually sunk into something like a calm, the great man arose on his legs, looked calmly yet dignified around him, worked his head in imitation of a bow several times, and was finally hoisted upon the table by a number of the members ; where in one hand flourishing his pipe, and in the other his queer and rather ventilating brimmer, he put forward one of his wooden pins in the most graceful attitude ; while with the other he occasionally thumped pretty loudly on the table in order that he might give force to his words; he spoke to the following beautiful effect :—

" My vorthy colleagys, this here is von o' th' most pleasantest tasks vot has ever comed to my lot since I fust took to th' cross ! (*Cheers.*) I am werry much revarded for all vot I have done in seein' o' so many 'spectable gemmen around me !—Here's all your jolly good healths!" (Here the celebrated man paused for a brief space of time, and taking up half a pint of " *Mountain Dew*," in the enthu-

siasm of the moment drank it off at a single swallow, which same noble action was rewarded by the unanimous plaudits of the delighted auditors ; breathless silence was then once more obtained, and the originator of the ' *Cadgers' Club,*' resumed as follows ;)—" Gemmen, although I am pertikerlerly modest, I must say that to me you are indebted for every blessin' vot yer now enjoys !" (*A great clatter of wooden legs.*) " I long beheld vith regret that the Cadgers' of London, vot ought to be a most 'spectable body o' people, vos werry much degraded by a parcel o' sneaks a gettin' into it, an' I seed plain enough that no good vos to be done vithout a union ! (*Loud cheers.*) It vos then that the glorious, the noble hidea occurred to me o' foundin' o' this 'sociation !—Yes, I took th' birch broom o' reformation into my fist, an' applying it to th' crossing o' corruption, I am proud an' happy to say that I have succeeded in cleansing the road of the muck, and that there is every prospect o' th' Cadgers' Club, becoming not only von o' th' most renowned, but 'spectable 'sciety's in th' vorld ! *(Cheers.)* Gemmen, I have nothin' more at present to add ; than to drink to von an' all yer good healths, an' to vish prosperity to yer in b'sness, an' bad luck to th' overseers an' th' Mendicity 'Sciety !"

To describe the rapture with which this address was received, would be a vain attempt, and the next moment the learned founder's head was buried in a bowl of punch, and the rest of the members applied themselves with redoubled zeal to the drink and their pipes. Several propositions were then made and carried, one of which was that in order to keep up the dignity of the club, pipes be entirely discarded, and nothing but cigars smoken by any one, under pain of a very heavy fine. Beer was also ordered to be entirely abolished. A vote of thanks was awarded to Long Jimmy, a skinny looking remnant of mortality, with a ghastly countenance, for the benefit he had already done the fraternity, by his introduction of a new description of sham hysterical fit, which was of much easier accomplishment than any that had been worked before, and more likely to delude the public. There were several new candidates for cadging honours; one wished to mount a pair of crutches; —another put in his vote for a wooden leg; a third had an ambition to go in the fit line, and to shew his qualifications for the same, went into half a dozen of different descriptions, much to the satisfaction of the company. A fourth, a gentleman's footman who had lost his character, applied, and was elected, and he being well acquainted with the names of most of the nobility and their family anecdotes, he was advised to turn begging letter impostor. It was then ordered from the chair, that the club assemble by seven o'clock the following evening, for the purpose of detailing adventures, and the business being announced to have concluded for that evening, mirth was ordered to have full sway. The lady cadgers' were now allowed to enter, and to join with the others in the revelry of the night. There was a most surprising strong muster of "poor families," ragged girls—who held the delicate situations of "mud-larks," match-sellers, dealers in boot-laces; and two or three cleanly clad women who sported a couple of *borrowed* infants each in their arms, and had "made up their mouths," by gammoning twins. The scene now assumed a most hilarious aspect;—The ladies were of the most agreeable dispositions imaginable, and were ready to do any thing in a minute, either to sing, dance, laugh, drink, or eat!—Crown bowls of punch, quarts of max, and various other beverages, vanished with most surprising rapidity, and then an indistinct murmur arose among the Members of the Club, which gradually swelled into a loud cry for the supper!—Upon this the learned chairman arose, and said :—

"Gemmen, I'm sorry I has to offer a 'pology to yer about th' scran, but th' vorthy cook being taken suddenly ill, th' turkies vot ve ordered cannot be cooked to night, but th' landlord has procured us a round o' beef, and ham an' weal instead, and trusts as how you'll make shift vith them !"

"Oh, oh, " simultaneously groaned the company, "beef, ham, and weal for gentlemen cadgers'! Shame! shame!"

"But mister chairman," said a wide awake looking young gentleman, with Newgate drops hanging to his shoulders, "is ve to have no pies, or custards arterwards ?"

The learned chairman replied in the negative to this question, upon which there was another groan even louder than the first, and a vote of censure was unanimously passed upon the superintendants of the victualling department forthwith. Notwithstanding all this, the supper made its appearance, and the attack upon it was so furious, that in less than a quarter of an hour there were no signs of such a meal having taken place. The company by this time were getting considerably merry; the men had all displayed their vocal abilities, and the females had warbled sweetly some of the most refined street ballards, when it was proposed that this being the first quarterly meeting of the Club, they should finish the entertainments with a ball !—This proposal was received with the most eager shouts, the tables were cleared out of the room, *Jack the Scraper*, was mounted on a high chair, with his fiddle in his hand, and the Terpsichorean amusements commenced with a splendid display between two young ladies', who gave a most characteristic sort of *Pas de deux*, composed of the double shuffles, the men melodiously beating time on the floor with their feet. This having lasted as long as the before mentioned young ladies had any breath in their bodies, they concluded amidst great applause, and then the whole of the company stood up, and "prepared for action." It was one of the most animated scenes that probably was ever witnessed, Almack's must have sunk into insignificance before it; the company having given the signal, Jack struck up the beautiful air of 'Dusty Bob,' and off struck the dancers with steam velocity, the learned founder of the society leading them on with a grace and spirit that were truly inimitable. It was really beautiful to see the two wooden legs of the distinguished Jeremiah moving and thumping in the dance; sometimes twirling in the air to the imminent hazard of poking out somebody's eye, and at another time descending whop upon some ladys' or gentleman's shoeless toe!—Then Jeremiah gave a little bit of performance worthy of the celebrated Duvernay, namely, holding up his left leg in his hand, and spinning round and round on his right with surprising velocity!—Sudden, however, was the unexpected stop which was put to that distinguished cadgers' interesting performance ; a crack was heard, followed by a half smothered exclamation, and the company turning towards the spot to discover the cause, beheld the mighty Jeremiah Jumper, stuck fast on the floor, his two wooden legs having broken in and wedged him as tight as a vice.

The most powerful sensation that can well be conceived was caused by this ludicrous and unexpected accident, but nothing could equal the magnanimous conduct of the great and stupendous hero of this renowned society on that very extraordinary occasion, no alarm, no confusion was at all depicted in the eccentric looking frontispiece of that most intelligent cadger, but while the rest of the members evinced the most praiseworthy solicitude for the welfare of the illustrious founder of their society, he calmly folded his arms, finding it totally impossible to extricate himself from the curious situation he was placed in, and looked with a most beneficent smile on his cadging brotherhood, as he uttered those remarkable words, so completely characteristic of his mysterious and witty disposition :—

"Never mind, my rum'uns ! Yer have no occasion to flurry yourselves ; yer see I've only been a havin' a little game of *leg in the hole* to myself."

At this most curious burst of genius, Jeremiah laughed, the remaider of the cadgers' laughed ; the ladies' highly applauded, and there was a general and unanimous flourish of quart pots, wooden legs, and birch brooms !—

There was a little excentricity attached to the renowned founder of the Cadgers' Club, which although it is by no means a solitary instance among gentlemen of his fraternity, we must divulge in the present stage of our narrative, in order that the reader may not be at all astonished at many little incidents which it will be our duty to reveal in the course of our very surprising and incomparable history, and in which the before-mentioned excentricity will be brought most conspicuously before them. Be it known then, that the learned Jeremiah Jumper, had a most extraordinary knack of indiscriminately accepting of any thing in the shape of beverage, no consequence who the tenderer might be ; in addition to which interesting propensity, he had likewise a very peculiar and truly original method of doing justice to the said libations, for he never failed to drain the contents of every measure offered to him, to the very dregs ; in consequence of this enthusiastic propensity to do ample justice to the offers of his friends, it may not be a matter of astonishment to our readers, that he became what is techinacally designated by many persons 'sublimated' a considerable time before any other person, and when the remarkable and indescribable gentleman was in that curious situation, he had a strange *penchant* to make his intrinsic humour more apparent; now it so happened, that on the important occasion we have the honour of particularizing, by way of a prelude to the spirit stiring and unexampled adventures, we shall bring before the public in the course of this story, that the learned Jeremiah, probably more then usually exhilarated by the first quarterly meeting of that distinguished association he had had the most extreme felicity of creating, had entered with even more than his customary energy into the spirit of the *spirits*, that were so liberally diffused among the members, and the consequence was that the great man felt himself peculiarly happy, and notwithstanding the offers of the members to release him from the situation he was placed in, he refused to be so liberated until he had first sung no less than twelve songs of the most splendid and refined description, all in praise of cadging, and recommending with a spirit worthy of the eminent vocalist who did such infinite honour to them, the most strenuous perseverance in the very fashionable and respectable art of imposing upon the " *greenhorns*," who are by courtesy denominated the public.

Printed & Published by E. LLOYD, 62, Broad Street, Holborn.

These poetical effusions, which were all written by the talented Jeremiah himself, would have done honour to that splendid author, ycelpt, the *Poet Laureate* of Little St. Andrew Street, usually employed by that truly eminent and aristocratic Publisher Pitts!—The illustrious founder of the Cadgers' Society having thus facetiously exhibited the exuberance of his mirth, was by the help of a saw extricated from the floor, and resumed his terpsichorean sports with more than his accustomed vivacity.

CHAPTER II.

THE INTEREST OF THIS MOST INTERESTING OF ALL INTERESTING NARRATIVES RAPIDLY INCREASES.

—THE WHOLE, TRUE, AND PARTICULAR ACCOUNT OF A MOST REMARKABLE INCIDENT, VIZ. THE CADGERS' CHRISTENING,—THE SECOND NIGHT'S MEETING OF THE CLUB; WITH ONE OF THE MOST CURIOUS HISTORIES THAT HAS EVER BEEN BEFORE PRESENTED TO THE READER, IN ANY SHAPE OR WORK EXTANT.

JUST at this particular and highly interesting period of our narrative, and when the ball had recommenced with renewed vigour, there was suddenly heard a loud knocking underneath the trap-door by which the company gained an entrance to this scene of their nocturnal assemblies, which caused a momentary pause in the festivity of the proceedings; the watchword was asked for, and given by the person outside the trap, which being raised, exhibited a most curious individual to the view of all present.

The individual who thus suddenly introduced himself into the society, was a tall black man, minus one eye and a leg, who luxuriated in a dingy brown long coat, embellished with sundry patches, and which in several places gave evident signs of the particular line of business he thought proper, or found most profitable, to follow—namely, a "*mud wolloper,*" *alias* a crossing-sweeper. He was also a member of the Cadgers' Club, and one who, by his able advocacy of the rights and privileges of the profession, was much prized and respected by his brethren. He had, for some cause or other, which we shall hereafter mention, absented himself on this very important evening, and his arrival now, therefore, was greeted with much enthusiasm.

"*Black-Berry,*" as the enlightened and sable mud-raker was characteristically denominated, was married to a lady of the same delicate and fashionable calling, with a white countenance, when it was suffered to be visible from beneath the dirt which generally covered it, and who figured at a "cross" in the aristocratic neighbourhood of Portland Place, with occasionally one borrowed infant at her back, and another in her arms, which never failed to excite the sympathy of the public to a pretty interesting tune. At times, however, she only sported "dummies," *i. e.* counterfeit infants, stuffed with straw, and by which there is a considerable traffic carried on by the vagrants of the metropolis.

Fair Polly, as this lady was called, in order to distinguish her from her dark husband, had been united just two years, when, to the delight of Black-Berry, she presented him with two of the prettiest mahogany kinchins that had probably ever been seen. This was an event of the deepest interest to the happy parents; but the extacy of the sable father was beyond all bounds, for two or three very important reasons; the first of which was, the immense pecuniary saving it would be to him, and the trouble it would take off his hands. Hiring infants was very expensive, and carrying dummies was very dangerous; but now they would have no occasion to incur the expense of the one, or to run the risk of the other, and Black-Berry consequently considered the birth of the dingy twins as a fortune to him.

Upon the occasion of their christening, Black-Berry had determined to have such a jollification as the polite purlieus of Bloomsbury had never before been honoured with; and cards of invitation were lavishly distributed among his friends, neighbours, and brethren of the profession. Preparations had for weeks been making on the most liberal scale; gallons of max had been stowed away for the occasion; poultry fattened; itinerant musicians engaged; and every thing that the most unbounded liberality and hospitality could dictate, or the most extensive pecuniary resources could provide; nothing, it was resolved, should be wanting to promote the good fellowship, joviality, and hilarity of "The Cadgers' Christening!"

One thing, however, happened rather unfortunate, and did somewhat interrupt the pleasures of that memorable day, which was that the parents had unintentionally fixed on the very day upon which the members of the "Honourable Society of Cadgers" could not attend; the first quarterly meeting of the club was appointed to take place in the evening, and the consequence was, that the whole of the day the learned founder and most of the members would be busily occupied in arranging their business for that most important occasion. The disappointment was very great; Black-Berry made the most ample apologies, but it was impossible to delay the interesting ceremony, in consequence of the very extensive preparations that had been made; however, the sable "knight of the *cross*" had made them all promise most faithfully that they would adjourn to the establishment in which he *hung out*, to supper, as soon as the business of the club had been settled. By some means or the other, however, the members were so exhilirated by the cheering reports of their first quarterly night, and the talented Jeremiah was so completely mystified by the potations he had (in the true *spirit* of sociality only) taken so frequently, that they entirely forgot Black-Berry's invitation, and it was to remind them of the same, and to inform them that supper was waiting that that celebrated personage made his appearance at so very unseasonable an hour.

Now it is known to our readers, that the learned members had already partaken of one supper, and it may be asked, what could they want with another. From any person who is not so thoroughly acquainted with the tastes, customs, and peculiarities of the cadgers as we undoubtedly are, this question would not at all be irrelevant; great indeed was the epicurean qualities of that most profound and distinguished body; besides, it may be remembered that they considered that they had in fact only partaken of a "*snack*;" and then the respect to which one of their brethren was entitled, would not suffer them to reject his invitation. Three cheers for Black-Berry were therefore immediately given, on the appearance of the mahogany knight, and long life and prosperity to the kinchins; the spirits were immediately transported down the gullets of the spongy-throated members, the meeting was adjourned till the following night, and it was immediately determined that they should every one of them accompany Black-Berry to his domicile, to do full justice to the christening of his offsprings.

The scene which followed could never be surpassed; the procession which was immediately formed, beggars all description!—Never was such universal delight evinced on any occasion which we remember. It may very well be conceived that not one of the learned individuals could be altogether *compos mentis*, after the unrestrained carousals they had indulged in for the last few hours past; therefore the noise they promised to make, denoted any thing but approaching to harmony to the peaceful and rural neighbourhood of Saint Giles'. However the procession, (for it was agreed *mem. con.* that they should go in state,

and as became their august society, to the residence of Black-Berry), was quickly arranged under the judicious auspices of the learned chairman! the members and the *fairer* branches of the fraternity formed themselves into couples, each individual flourishing with conscious pride and delight, some trophy of their profession, a wooden leg; a birch broom; a pair of crutches; or a beggar's dress; *Jack the Scraper* led the way, bringing forth tones from his violin, that would have put even the great Paganini himself to the blush, had that very celebrated cat-gut torturer have ever had the presumption to attempt the refined and polite airs of "Bobs in the Watch-house," "Polly put the Kettle on," and others of equal sublimity!— After this gentleman, followed the very mighty and learned originator of this very talented society, the great Jeremiah Jumper himself, supported on the shoulders of two of the members, the great man being too much overpowed by his feelings, the delapidated state of his wooden supporters, and the strength of the good things he had taken, to walk. The appearance of that immortal King of the Cadgers was one of the most impressive description, his benignant countenance glimmered brightly from beneath its natural mud in the gas-light, with good humour and sensibility! In one hand he flourished one of his wooden legs, and in the other he held a quart pot, part of the contents of which he sometimes deposited down his own throat, and a portion on the heads of those who supported him; the learned man seemed almost above all human things, and bawled with stentorian might, the expression of his pleasurable emotions! The *ladies* were in the most delightful state that can well be imagined; and danced and jumped, if not in the most graceful, certainly in the most industrious manner.

In this *order*, if the term may be applied with any justice to the riotous and disorderly troop we are describing, the procession issued from the "snuggery," and in the most *imposing* manner, they wended their way to the beautiful 'spot in which the "bug walk" of Black-Berry was located. Three most tremendous shouts burst from them all when they gained the street, and the musician having struck up a most exciting tune, the Cadgers danced joyfully on their road to the scene of festivity, shouting, singing, and laughing!—The nocturnal prowler looked on and marvelled; quiet and honest tradesmen in High-street, popped forth their [night-cap-surmounted heads from their attic windows, and others came down from the said attics in their night clothes, shivering with cold, and thinking nothing less than that it was either an insurrection or that their habitations were on fire; watchmen sprung their rattles, and wisely fastened themselves in their watch-boxes, for they dared not interfere with that powerful and truly illustrious body. It is a well known fact that Saint Giles's and other back slums, are quite worthy of the title of separate states, for the inhabitants of them at all times act precisely as their own feelings dictate, and their inclinations prompt them, without any fear of the interference of the strong arm of the law;—feel they inclined for the innocent amusement of a general mill, they give the most unrestrained indulgence to their propensity, and where is the whole legion of policemen who would venture to interrupt them. Every rookery is a fortress well stored with implements for the roughest part of warfare, and plenty of fearless young *gentlemen* who know uncommonly well how to use them, and it needs but a signal, which same signal need only be the appearance of an officer in an hostile manner, and the whole inhabitants of the desperate territory will immediately rush to action and deal destruction around them. This is no exaggerated picture of life as it is, in the *back slums*, but such as it precisely is, and which can be authenticated on the most unquestionable authority. In the course of our remarkable history, we shall have occasion to give the most minute details of every haunt, rookery, corner, and retreat in the metropolis, with such particulars of the doings in them, and the characters visiting them, that we do not hesitate in saying will not only render the Papers of the *Cadgers' Club*, a work of the most infinite, incomparable, and irresistible

humour, but at the same time a record of some of the most curious and astounding occurrences of fact, that has ever before been submitted to perusal.

Having thus taken the liberty of digressing from the subject we were so graphically describing, we must apologize, and resume our story. The particulars we have just mentioned being known to the reader, he can very easily account for the watchmen preferring the springing of their rattles in the snug retreat of their watch-boxes to their openly and valiantly interfering with the members of the Cadgers' Club to reduce them to decent order and decorum: and we shall not detain the, no doubt, impatient reader longer than is absolutely necessary, by any useless detail, but at once bring the procession to the door of Black-Berry's fashionable ken, in Lawrence-street, Bloomsbury, where they arrived after full half an hour's perambulation around the neighbourhood.

What a beautiful, romantic, and picturesque street is Lawrence-street, Bloomsbury! Lovely retreat of cadgers, costermongers, bricklayer's labourers, no labourers at all, fences and pickpockets! Lawrence-street is the very Arcadia, the complete Elysium of Saint Giles's! Salubrious are the spots, pleasant the streets, and beautiful the scenes around the classic regions of Seven Dials, of Chick Lane, and Whitechapel, but oh, how dull, how sad, how common they all appear to Lawrence-street, Bloomsbury! Ease and liberality are in the elegant, yet careless arrangement of its tottering houses, with their broken roofs, and glassless casements! If there is a spot in the world that is free from the demon called aristocracy, that spot must assuredly be Lawrence-street! Oh, it is a delightful spot, dear to prigs and cadgers from time immemorial! Happy must be its inmates; no cares of rent disturb their mind; they cannot " *take up their bed and walk,*" for the " rope " generally supplies them with the means of repose! They cannot die of melancholy through the loneliness of their situation, for some fifty always repose in one room together, in the most happy state of conviviality! Such

then is Lawrence-street, the street which had the honour of giving a shelter to Black-Berry, and which was fated on the night we are speaking of, to be the scene of the greatest hilarity that was ever before registered in the annals of mirth! Six loud and long-continued huzzas, announced to the persons who were within the domicile of Black-Berry that the immortal society of the Cadgers had arrived to do them honour, and soon they made their appearance at the street-door, and in the warmest and most enthusiastic manner, welcomed them! The mighty Jeremiah was taken from the shoulders of those who had hitherto had the honour of bearing him, and, amid the most tumultous manifestations of delight, was carried up the stairs, followed by the remainder of the learned members of the club.

The scene which was exhibited to the view upon the entrance of the Society, baffles all description! The room in which this interesting scene of festivity was held, was a very large one, with very few articles of furniture, and those articles it did contain, were in such a mutilated state, that it would puzzle many persons to conceive for what purpose they had been originally intended. There were a few chairs without backs, and some minus bottoms, and one or more of the legs; and those who had been unsuccessful in obtaining that accomodation, had betaken themselves to the floor, to the bottoms of old tubs, or any other substitute for a chair that they could lay their hands upon. The company, which was of the same heterogeneous quality which had lately honoured the "Snuggery," were in a state of considerable excitement upon the entrance of the members, for most of them declared they were remarkably "peckish," having delayed the supper until they arrived; while others expressed their fears that the poultry would be cold, and some were fearful that their appetite would fail them, it being past the time at which they usually supped. Some were smoking; some were joking, and all were drinking most extravagantly. In one corner was an amorous couple of match venders, the lady's mouth embellished with a short pipe, enjoying themselves with a dance *a la* Dusty Bob and Black Sal, and in another was a *blind* beggar *blind drunk*, stretched at full length upon the floor.

The room was thickly and abundantly besprinkled with feminines, who paid the most profound attention to those of the other sex. One was expressing her most unqualified contempt for those females "*what*" would submit to the vulgar profession of millinery, dress-making, or straw bonnet-building when there was such a respectable, lucrative, and fashionable calling as those they followed !—Another was complaining most bitterly of the awful falling off in the match trade, and as an alarming proof of the same, declared that she had *only* taken one pound thirteen shillings that day. This young lady's countenance looked most awfully melancholly as she gave utterance to this account, and her companions looked almost incredulously upon her. At one end of the room, mounted upon an old table, were three musicians, who blew forth strains that sounded only like the growling of so many wild beasts in a menagerie, but which the company all expressed their entire approbation of, and applauded most vocifernosly and clamourously. The room was lighted by several long and miserable looking candles; some stuck in tin sticks, and others in old blacking bottles, or clay candlesticks of the most elegant and choice construction !—There was a large barrel of "heavy" in one corner of the room, at the cock of which a young gentleman was applying his mouth most industriously unnoticed by the company, who were too busily occupied in other affairs. The large table in the centre of the room, at which only the most favoured guests were seated, was densly crowded with gin measures, pots, cans, pipes, and tobacco; and from the zeal with which each individual applied himself to them, it was very evident that not one of them would escape being done full honour to.

No sooner was the immortal and benevolent founder of "The Cadgers' Club," brought into the room, than the guests all started to their feet, and loud shouts of "Jumper! Jumper! Jerry!" shook the roof of the mansion ! Glasses were charged, and the health of our hero was drank in the most enthusiastic manner possible. It was a glorious moment of that great man's life, and he felt it sensibly; being mounted on a fresh pair of wooden pins, three times did he attempt to utter his gratitude; but, alas ! words were denied him, and he finally relinquished the attempt, and suffered himself to be carried to the head of the table, and placed in a chair, on the right hand side of that which was intended for the occupation of the worthy hostess, Mrs. Berry ! Black-Berry took his seat on the left, and then Mrs. Berry made her appearance with the two mahogany pledges of her spouse's affection in her arms, which were introduced to Mr. Jumper; and the other Cadgers, who all performed the ceremony of re-christening them, namely, by sprinkling their faces with a decent quantity of "The Elixir of Life !" This ceremony having been performed amidst the loudest acclamations of all present; the supper was at last brought smoking hot upon the table, to the evident satisfaction of every one present. We shall not seek to pourtray in language, what was done by the industrious jaws of every one at the table, and those who for want of room, were compelled to be content with the floor; suffice it to say that they each proved themselves the most expert gourmands, and those individuals who had already partaken of such a plenteous repast at "the Snuggery," ate with even greater voracity than those who had not eaten any other meal for several hours. The toasts given were of the most original and clever description, and long life and prosperity to the "little dears," was not forgotten to be drunk no less than twenty times, "upstanding uncovered," and with the most vehement applause.

A Cadger's meal is never of any lengthy description, for they have a most extraordinary method of despatching the largest quantity in the shortest time; the viands were therefore very quickly masticated; the table was cleared; the lush vessels replenished; pipes were resumed, and harmony commenced, by the learned and honourable Jeremiah Jumper, Esq. condescending to warble in the most dulcet, hurdy-gurdy notes, the annexed beautiful production, which we think our readers will acknowledge is by far superior to any thing that has ever been written by the celebrated Johnny Morgan, of Cat-nachian and Pittonian noteriety. The learned gentleman, in addition to the beautiful tones played by the musicians, had a style of his own in accompanying himself on the floor of the room with the stump of his wooden pin, and his companions lent their aid in the chorus, by not only bawling to the full extent of their lungs, but also by working with their hands and elbows, the imaginary clacking of a windmill, a sort of performance peculiar to individuals of their *elevated* station of life.

THE CADGERS' SONG!

Mankind you will own are as artful as
    badgers,
No matter our rank, we are ev'ry one
    cadgers;
From our birth 'tis a maxim instill'd in
    in our mind,
Do our best to go first, let who will come
    behind,
    Then whate'er folks may say, they're
      all artful as badgers,
    And whatever their station, they're all
      of them cadgers!

The child is a cadger,—for both girls
    and boys,
They cadge on their parents for fruit,
    cakes, and toys;
The lass is a cadger,—although you may
    start,
She goes cadging about for some young
    fellow's heart.
          Then whate'er, &c.

The tradesman's a cadger, for credit he
    begs,
Puts each one in the hole,—then he
    takes to his legs;
The M. P's. a cadger of infinite grace,
He cadges for votes, just to get into
    place.
          Then, whate'er, &c.

The lawyer's a cadger, who causes you
    grief,
He goes cadging about just to get a
    brief,
The bishop's a cadger—a worse can't be,
He opens folks *eyes* just to get him a *see*.
          Then whate'er, &c.

Good luck to the man who to cadge first
    began,
For to do without cadging no person
    now can,
We're all of us cadgers in this world
    below;
Then success unto cadging wherever we
    go!
    Then whate'er folks may say, they're
      all artful as badgers,
    No matter their station, I've proved
      they're all cadgers!

The deafening shouts of applause, the stamping of feet, the rattling of crutches, and all the other usual demonstrations of pleasure which followed this truly splendid display of vocal and poetical genius, continued to shake the room for several minutes, which had the most visable effect upon the learned and sensitive Jeremiah; but his modesty made him feel abashed, and to hide his confusion, he secreted his head behind the apron of Mrs. Berry, and applying a pot full of gin to his lips, he composed his spirits with a comfortable draught in private.

The harmony so well began, proceeded with great spirit, Mr. Jumper's admirable effort being followed by a sentimental ballad by a young gentleman cadger with straight hair, and a sedate countenance, who was well known about the metropolis as a chaunter of hymns, being usually accompanied by a young woman to represent his wife, and two or three children, all very respectably attired. After this song had been duly sung, chorused, and applaused, Black Berry exhibited his musical powers by sing the duet of "All's Well," with his wife, after which every other person sung, and then the dancing began, which it was intended to keep up till daylight.

While the latter sport was going on, and Black-Berry was amusing the company with a dance after the manner of the wild Indians, the enlightened founder of the Cadgers' Club, who did not feel disposed to dance, devoted his sole attention and conversational powers to Mrs. Berry, who had also declined the Terpsichorean sports! Barring a squint, the loss of half her nose, and being *rather* dirty, Mrs. Berry was a most fascinating woman! The susceptible, the learned Mr. Jumper had a heart as big as a paving stone, and can it be wondered that it should melt beneath the sweet accents, the fiery squint, and delicate features of Mrs. Berry, or that that truly beautiful woman, when she gazed on the benevolent countenance of Mr. Jumper, and then removed her glances to the muddy countenance of her *cara sposa*, should be captivated?

It may be urged that the noble soul of Jeremiah should have scorned the idea of trying to seat himself in the affections of another man's wife; and that Mrs. Berry ought to have remembered her mahogany offsprings, and spurned the thought of betraying the author of their being; but alas! the power of love is well known, and the beings we are now speaking of were, besides, too susceptible of its power! Long had they pledged each other in silence; then followed whispers, sighs, and every other delicious little preliminary; and had not the unconscious Black-Berry have been too much occupied in the dance to pay the least attention to any thing else, he might have heard two or three of the most beautiful kisses, which were enough to inflame a stoic's heart. Too soon, however, the hapless black cadger was aroused from his apathy; suddenly turning round, and looking towards the spot where the amorous couple had just been seated, he exclaimed:—

"Why, bere Massa Jumper?"

The company all stared amazed, but said not a word; two or three had noticed the very amiable terms upon which the learned cadger and Mrs. Berry had seemed together, and had their suspicions, which they wisely kept to themselves.

In the meantime, Black-Berry's large optics rolled fiercely round the apartment, as he discovered that his rib was missing as well as the founder of the club.

"An' bere Missee Berra?" cried the astonished black; "she be berry mush 'gaged wib Massa Jumper jus'a now!"

"Trifles light as air,
Are, to the jealous, confirmations strong
As proofs of holy writ!"

And, as the most bewildering and distracting thoughts shot across the brain of the disturbed black; his confused countenance looked for all the world like an immense black pudding in convulsions! The dancing was immediately stopped, and Black-Berry called wildly upon the name of his lovely wife, but no one answered, and his horror increased! He beat his breast, tore the wool off his head, and exhibited various other symptoms of temporary mental derangement; but at last he seemed to recollect himself, and rushed towards a low door at the further end of the apartment, that gave admittance to a small snoozing crib, which was furnished with a considerable quantity of clean straw, and which Black-Berry let out on hire at the enormous sum of twopence per night, each sleeper.

First he placed his ear to the key-hole —distraction! he heard sighs, kisses and whispers!—Then he placed his eye to the key-hole;—madness! There he beheld almost a confirmation of his worst surmises; his wife and Jeremiah were together; the latter throwing himself into a variety of impressive attitudes, expressive of the very strong passion he had imbibed for the better half of Black-Berry.

"Love-ly hangil!" the enraged black heard him repeat, "hif I could only take off my pegs, I vould go down on my stumps to tell how much I love yer!"

Mrs. Berry sighed, and squinted a most fascinating look of approval upon Jeremiah! First she advanced her hand —then she offered her cheek; this was too much for the tender hearted founder of the Cadgers' Club, and enfolding the yielding beauty in a most ardent embrace, he pressed the most affectionate kisses upon her lips! The distracted black man could endure no more; all the time he had been looking on this scene, his eyes had been rolling about like two balls of cobbler's wax in a basin of cream,

With one kick of his wooden leg he burst open the door of the room, and exposing the guilty pair to the gaze of the wondering spectators, he exclaimed, in a voice choked with wrath, "Dam vhite rascal!"

The next moment he had pinned the celebrated Jeremiah to the wall with his wooden peg, and Jeremiah had returned the compliment by a similar action in the stomach of the enraged black. Mrs. Berry bawled her utmost, and commenced a furious attack on the ball of worsted belonging to her spouse, while the company looked on, and seemed to enjoy the scene vastly.

There is not a more curious and in-

teresting display, than a fight between two wooden legged men. The action commences with the grand thrust, namely, pinning each other against the wall, as we have already described; then follows a wrestling match in which the object is to attempt to break one anothers legs, and then bring them to the ground and to the mercy of their adversary, but if either of those scientific movements fail, the rule is for the combatants each placing their backs against a wall, to remove one of their legs, which they convert into an instrument of defence, and the combat is renewed with redoubled vigour and determination. All these various methods of fighting were

No. 3.

put into force, by the hero of these pages and the jealous black, and dreadful was the strife which for some time raged between them.

We are not so egotistical as to pretend to give any thing like an accurate description of the scene which followed this most awful and sanguinary affray; twice did the chivalrous Jeremiah bring his sable adversary to the ground, and twice did the no less heroic Black Berry pin the immaculate founder of "*The Cadgers' Club*" like a cockchafer against the wall; driving what small portion of wind that was left in Jeremiah's unhappy body, completely out of it, and as he figuratively expressed himself, "giving him *bellus* to mend!" Yet still was the courage of the fierce combatants unabated, and it was quite uncertain when the frightful and bloody engagement would have terminated, had it not been for the harsh but opportune interference of the too tender-hearted Mrs. Berry, who came to the assistance of our hero, wielding with terrific gestures a quart pot, with which she proceeded immediately to try the quality of her hapless spouse's pericranium, by bringing him to the floor with tremendous violence. The contest, although one of the principal combatants was thus brought *hors de combat*, now assumed a more alarming aspect than ever; some of the young lady's of the " Cross," and two or three of the " matchless," fraternity, who had a sneeking regard for the ebony cadger, began to remonstrate sharply against the brutal treatment of his wife; others took the part of Mrs. Berry, then the " gentlemen" of the young ladies who felt indignant at the conduct of Mrs. Berry, took up the cause of their fair lovers; and the respectable swains of the opposite party, of course stood forth to fight the cause of their favourites! words of the least delicate description in the world were freely bestowed, and as liberally returned; general confusion followed; threats were poured fourth most plentifully, then followed a general wielding of pots, pokers, crutches, chairs, sticks, and every implement that could be obtained; there was one simultaneous shout, it was the signal for a general mill, and the next moment nothing was

to be heard but the terrific din of war ! The women screamed—the men bawled and swore ;—heads cracked, a torrent of pewter flew about in all directions, and never was heard or seen such a terrific battle before. All Lawrence Street was up in arms; while all the cadgers who had assembled for the purpose of celebrating the birth of the offsprings of Black Berry, were receiving *harms* from one another.

How the chivalrous Jeremiah Jumper might have distinguished himself, what valiant deeds he might have achieved, we are in no situation to offer an idea, as unfortunately for that learned gentlemen, he was rendered totally incapable of doing any thing at all, he being buried beneath an immense heap of mutilated combatants, who having fallen upon the floor, were embracing each other most affectionately, and doing a little bit of performance peculiar to themselves, which was the refined and delicate wit of *buttling* one another with their heads, and in some instances doing a small bit of cannibalism, namely, by devouring, or decapitating each other's noses !—As for the unfortunate Black Berry, he had become insensible from the effects of the affectionate attack of his wife, and was stretched at full length upon the floor, environed by at least half a dozen other wounded and insensible cadgers ! At length, however, each person apparently having what is technically called had " his belly full," the battle ceased; the meeting was broke up, and slowly dispersed, silence once more reigned in the romantic and peaceful purlieus of Lawrence Street, and thus terminated the Cadger's Christening.

We have been at some trouble to endeavour to elicit the particulars of the conduct of Jeremiah and Black Berry after the termination of this affray, whether they were restored to their sences on that morning, and whether the tender and considerate Mrs. Berry attended to their wants, and forgot her own aroused feelings in the painful situation of her better half and his rival, and endeavoured to bring them to an amicable arrangement. But we must confess that there is a great deal of mystery attached to this portion of our important narrative, to which we have not been enabled to find any elucidation either from the documents of the society, or the lips of the illustrious founder of the club himself. We have indeed from another quarter been informed, but mind, reader, we do not offer to vouch for its authenticity, that Black Berry was found in the same insensible situation at daylight; and that just at break of day there was seen to issue from the mansion of the sable knight of the cross, a figure remarkably like that of the celebrated Mr. Jumper, while at the same moment, a face emerged from a broken square of glass in the front attic, which bore a great resemblance to that which was the sole property of Mrs. Berry, and stretching itself far over the parapet, looked unutterable things at the learned founder of the Cadgers' Club, as he quickly "*cut his wood*" from the polite and elegant neighbourhood of Lawrence Street, Bloomsbury.

But the painful occurrence we have been so particular in narrating, was not fated to rest there; the feelings of the susceptible black crossing-purifier were exasperated; his heart was wounded—his honour was touched; for as "there is honour among thieves," so is there the same degree of honour amongst cadgers—at least it was the case with Black-Berry. He felt that his *reputation* had been aimed at by the too gallant founder of the Cadgers' Society; that he had basely abused his friendship and brought to ruin the connubial happiness he had hitherto enjoyed, for ever, and he burned for vengeance! No sooner had he recovered his senses, than he determined to challenge Jeremiah to mortal combat. This resolution he immediately put into execution, and just as the immortal Jeremiah was about to depart in the morning upon his usual business, he was arrested in his progress by a little grimey-faced boy, without shoes or stockings, who proved to be the Mercury of Black-Berry, and delivered into the hands of Jeremiah, a greasy and dirty paper, folded into something between the size and shape of a letter and a parcel, on the face of which was inscribed, in curious hieroglyphical sort of characters, "*Tow Gerrymier Jumper, Eskwyer!*" The re-

nowned hero of these pages unfolded this elegantly written and indicted epistle, and after ten minutes' hard spelling, was enabled to make out that it was a challenge from his injured adversary of the previous night, appointing to meet him at three o'clock in the afternoon of that day, "if the vether permits," in a certain street, and with the usual implements, to decide their quarrel in honorable combat!

Perhaps one of the drollest and most peculiar scenes that can be witnessed, is an "affair of honour" among the knights of the broom; and as our readers are, doubtless, most of them unacquainted with the fun of such an affair, we shall take the liberty of minutely describing a cadgers' combat, or a crossing-sweepers' duel!

It is an invariable rule among the members of the crossing-sweepers' association, of which it will be scarcely credited there are at the present day innumerable societies, to combine together for the purpose of scouting and punishing any impudent intruder upon what they consider their rights; in other words, to use the most effectual means of putting to the rout any individual who may have taken to himself a "cross" without being duly elected and rendered a free man to pursue his professional duties. No sooner is it known to one of the "knights of the cross," as the mud-dispersers of the metropolis appropriately denominate themselves, that a stranger has made a stand at any crossing where the *mopusses* are likely to be picked up, than it is communicated by him to his muddy brethren, and they appoint a day and hour to repair in a body to the same delinquent's place of business, and to punish him for his presumption. A wet and muddy day is generally fixed upon, and each gentleman sweeper carries his birch with him, and hastening in a body of perhaps a dozen, they first reason with the intruder on the dishonesty of his proceedings, in thus injuring the rights and *respectability* of the profession, and demand that he immediately quit the place he has invaded, and agree to pay a fine amounting to a leg-of-mutton supper, and promise to offend no more until he is duly initiated into all the secrets privileges and rules of the society.   If the offender has the temerity to refuse to accede to such demands, the signal for desperate measures is immediately given, each knight of the cross buries his birch in a profusion of soft mud, and in an instant the unhappy interloper is half smothered in mire, beat to the ground, and severely drubbed with the brooms of the knights, until he is as awful a sample of a mud-lark as can well be imagined. This method of proceeding seldom fails to have the desired effect, that of either scouting the offender, or of inducing him to pay the fine, and enter into the society; and if he is obstinate, and continues to monopolize the cross, the dose is repeated till he is fairly reduced to submission.   This is no overcharged picture of the doings of these fellows; during the life of the late Sir Richard Birnie, four crossing-sweepers were brought before him, on a charge of thus maltreating a poor wretch who, from being a respectable tradesman in the neighbourhood of Oxford-street, was reduced to the dreadful necessity of taking to a crossing at the corner of Berner's-street. When the poor fellow appeared at the office, it was impossible scarcely to distinguish in him either the features or figure of a human being, so completely had he been encrusted with mud from the revengeful brooms of the knights of the cross! The leader of these fellows had the impudence to request Sir Richard to inflict a fine upon them, or to suffer them to settle it with the plaintiff; this was of course refused, and they were each of them committed for three months, to hard labour, as rogues and vagabonds, and for the assault upon the plaintiff. On searching them, there was found upon their persons a sum amounting to no less than four pounds in copper and sixpences, which they acknowledged they had made from a few hours' "work" in the morning!

Having thus minutely described the above facts, it may only be deemed necessary to inform our readers, that all *affairs of honour*, as the aristocratic portion of the public think proper to denominate an hostile meeting, are settled among the *mud wollopers* in a similar manner.   The duellists meet at an appointed place, where there is known to be a good collection of mud, armed only with their brooms, and belabour and bemire each other, till one declares he has had enough, when the business is settled, and is generally finished by a good *blow out* at one of their nocturnal meeting-houses.

The courageous, the chivalrous, the martial, the honourable, and the invincible spirit of the distinguished Jeremiah must already have been made apparent to the readers of this wonderful history; it will therefore be no matter of surprise to them then, when we say that no sooner had the learned secretary read the daring letter of Black-Berry, than he resolved to give him every means of satisfaction.   He delivered a message to that effect, to the before mentioned grimey-faced and shoeless Mercury, and fixed upon a convenient spot not far from the classic regions of Battle Bridge as the place of meeting. This point being settled, Jeremiah immediately hastened to the daily house of call for the *respectable* portion of the Cadgers, namely, the far-famed "Sheep's Head Tavern," Little Saint Andrew Street, Seven Dials, where he communicated the particulars of the challenge he had received, and appointed his seconds and umpires. The day turned out a lovely one for the decision of the combat;—the rain poured down a perfect deluge, and the mud accumulated in gratifying heaps in every street.   After having duly refreshed their insides with sundry and innumerable "yards of tape," the distinguished party issued from the Sheep's Head Tavern, shouldering their brooms, and bent their way towards the place of appointment. Desperation and the most undaunted courage were displayed in every feature, every gesture, and every action of the great and valarous founder of the Cadger's Club, as at the head of his gallant companions he marched, shouldering his broom, and whistling aloud in the most mellifluous notes that beautiful and popular production entituled and called "Barbary Allen."

The ancient bell of the ancient church of Saint Pancras, chimed the hour of three exactly, as Mr. Jumper and his

valiant companions arrived at the scene of action, which was a dull, muddy, and unfrequented street, somewhere adjacent to the Small-pox Hospital. The distinguished Jeremiah looked with an eye of the most unbounded satisfaction upon the river of soft mud which so tranquilly glided along the centre of the road, and in the kennels of the street; and then he turned round to his companions, and expressed his impatience for the arrival of his adversary. They had, however, not long to wait, for in a few minutes afterwards, Black-Berry shouldering his birch, and followed by half a dozen more of his friends, was seen to turn the corner of the street, and advance towards our hero, and there was a look of determination in the ebony features of that deeply injured man, which shewed plain enough that he was fully resolved to come to no amicable arrangements until he had fully avenged his wounded honour; and there was a glance of sanguinary and ghastly purport in the white of his saucer ogles, which to any one but a person possessed of the invincible courage of Mr. Jumper, would have struck the greatest terror; but Jeremiah, the truly courageous Jeremiah, beheld it

all with the utmost indifference, and there was a resolute movement in his wooden legs, that seemed to say, as plainly as words could have spoken, " I'll have a shy, if I lose my *stick*."

Black-Berry and his friends having arrived at the spot, a dead pause of a second or two ensued, during which interval the duelists eyed each other with the most awful presaging looks of anniliation, and then the seconds of Black-Berry spoke to the sekonds of Mr. Jumper, and desired to know whether he was willing to offer up a public apology to the " *gentleman*," he had so deeply injured, at the meeting of their society in the evening. This question being put by his seconds to Mr. Jumper, that magnanimous individval spurned it with well merited contempt, and preparations were accordingly immediately made for commencement of the combat. Each combatant was alowed to choose his favorite heap of mud, and the distance being marked, they planted their brooms deeply in the mire, and resting their arms upon the handles of them, looked fiercely and terrificaly in each others countenances, eagerly awaiting the signal to commence the combat. This was a moment of the most painful and indescribable suspense, not a lip was seen to move, not a breath or a whisper disturbed the dead, and realy painful stillness of that interval. At length, however, the signal was given by the seconds throwing their hats up in the air, and the same instant the immaculate Mr. Jumper had planted his birch loaded with soft mud, plump in the sable frontispiece of Black-Berry, filling the mouth, eyes, and nostrils of that unfortunate gentleman, with mud, and effectually preventing him returning the compliment on his own person for a minute or two. A deafening shout arose from the seconds and friends of our hero, upon this wonderful and valiant achievement and that celebrated personage being too wise to neglect the advantage he had thus gained, flourished his overwhelming birch about with such courageous skill, that he lodged a considerable portion of the mud which had been in the road, on the person of his rival, before that sable knight had even had half a chance of defending himself. Jeremiah, seeing the painful situation of his rival, with that nobleness of mind for which he is immortalized, desisted for a few seconds, and resting on the handle of his broom, generously awaited the recovery of Black-Berry from his confusion! At length the sable cadger, having succeeded in partially cleansing the mud from his large optics, and after spitting forth almost enough mud to fill a scavenger's cart, fixed one stern look upon our hero, which proved the desperate state of his courage, and after some clever manœuvering on both sides, the combat was renewed with admirable valour. In this round, the founder of the Cadgers' Society came in for a pretty fair share of the mud, but he ultimately succeeded in flooring the hapless Black-Berry plump into a large heap of the most delicious filth they could have desired for such an occasion, and then kindly finished his business by sweeping an immense flood of mire over him, so as to completely hide his body from the view. The umpires now declared that Jeremiah was the victor; and the unfortunate black, having been extricated from his *rather* unpleasant situation,

when he had found the power of speech declared that he was perfectly *satisfied,* shook hands with his conqueror, and was then immediately taken to a pump, which novel sort of shower-bath had, in a short time, the effect of restoring him and his late antagonist to something of their pristine purity. This business being accomplished, the whole party hastened to a flash "slum" in the neighbourhood, and, over a quart or two of the most incomparable *stream of chrystal,* in less than an hour became as good friends as if the circumstance had not taken place at all.

CHAP. III.

THE SECOND NIGHT'S GRAND AND MEMORABLE MEETING OF THE CADGERS' CLUB.—COMMENCEMENT OF THE TALES AND ADVENTURES OF THE MEMBERS.—THE LIFE, VICISSITUDES, TRICKS, PERILS, AND MARVELLOUS EXPLOITS OF A CADGER; FORMING ONE OF THE MOST SURPRISING, USEFUL, AND INTERESTING NARRATIVES EVER WRITTEN—FULL OF WIT, HUMOUR, AND MIRACULOUS ADVENTURE.

HAVING thus sufficiently introduced the reader to the characters who will so prominently figure in this work, and given them a pretty fair sample, we presume of the fun they may expect to be detailed in the course of our very remarkable history; we shall proceed without any further digression to the more immediate objects of our design, and to put them into possession of the particulars of the second night's meeting of the learned members of the Cadgers' Club, and also to make them acquainted with perhaps one of the most curious and romantic episodes, that was ever before presented to the public.

No sooner had the hour appointed for the assembling of the Club, chimed from the steeple of Saint Giles' church, then the Cadgers' Snuggery was thronged with its learned members, and the distinguished and amiable Mr. Jumper was seen at his usual post, gazing upon all around him, with the utmost placidity, and exhibiting no symptoms of the terrific fray, he had been engaged in in the afternoon. There was an unusual strong muster of the members assembled on this occasion, the utmost interest and curiosty being excited by the previous night's announcement, that on this occasion one of the members would commence the first of a series of narratives which were ordered to be communicated by the members, for their general benefit, instruction, and amusement, and the business of the Club having been quickly settled, and the supper despatched, glasses were replenished, pipes were loaded, and they proceeded to cast lots to know upon whom the task should devolve to relate the particulars of his life; the chance fell upon one of the oldest persons in that important society, who was known by the somewhat quaint and felicitous cognomen of "*Scapegrace Jack!*" This individual was a tall respectably clad, and respectable visaged personage; who was upwards of seventy years of age, and had retired from the more bustling vocations of a Cadgers' life, to the peaceful enjoyment of a sum amounting to no less than six thousand pounds, the whole of which he had managed to accumulate, by levying contributions on the gullibility of the public in various well imagined and equally well executed stratagems. He was a man who possessed an intellect, which rendered him capable, had his inclinations corresponded with it, of becoming one of the brightest ornaments of society, and he bore the stamp of a man who had experienced much, thought deeply, but acted improvidently. To the society, he was one of its best friends, and strange it may appear, "*Scapegrace Jack,*" although a man so far superior to any of the common herd of cadgers' who flocked to the "Snuggery," in point of mind, seemed to think it the very acme of pleasure and intellectual enjoyment to be in the society of its members. No sooner was this individual's name announced, as the one on whom the lot had fallen, to begin those wonderful tales, which will be found so plenteously strewn throughout the pages of this

work, than there was a sumultaneous shout of applause, which made the "Snuggery," shake again, and the learned Mr. Jumper having got up on his pins with much dignity, yet suavity of manner, and in a very neat speech, congratulated the members of the club, on their unexpected good fortune in being thus, on the first night of the historical proceedings of the society, ordained to be delighted with the exploits and adventures, of one of the most venerable, and certainly one of the most respectable members of that distinguished association; and Mr. Jumper, having concluded an impressive and eloquent harrangue, highly complimentary to "Scapegrace Jack," *sat down,* and the beforementioned "Scapegrace Jack" *stood up.* In a moment there was a profound silence, and the learned and noble individual before alluded to, prefaced his wonderful story by the following address :—

"Gentlemen, members of the most distinguished and honourable Society of the Metropolitan Street Cadgers, it having fallen to my lot to be the first to relate my adventures, I beg leave to prepare you to hear a narrative of varied, curious, and marvellous construction, a narrative which in many parts may appear so truly romantic, and improbable, that you might feel inclined to doubt my veracity, were I not ready previous to my commencing it, to state my *honour,* as a gentleman and a cadger, for the authenticity of all I shall state. Mine has been a life from which much may be learnt both intellectually and professionally, and I particularly call the attention of those persons to it, who have but lately entered on the *honourable,* interesting, and ingenious profession of vagrancy, or, more properly speaking, cadging; by listening attentively to my chequered life, they will be made acquainted with a few artful moves, which cannot fail to be of use to them in their business, which may even be new to old experienced Cadger's, and by which I have been enabled to accumulate a handsome fortune!"

With this brief, but appropriate exordium, "Scapegrace Jack" sat down amidst great applause; took a hearty swig at a tumbler of port wine negus, which was standing before him, and relighting his pipe, placed himself in a situation where he could be distinctly heard by every one, and after a brief space of time, during which he seemed to be collecting and arranging his reminisances, he commenced his singular narrative in the following words :—

THE AUTOBIOGRAPHY OF "SCAPE-GRACE JACK."

From the secret Papers of the Cadgers' Club.

" It is now as near as I can recollect about sixty years ago, since I found myself one of the inmates of a wretched hovel, situated near that most dreary and extensive heath called *Black Hammilton*, which occupies a distance of twenty one miles, destitute alike of tree, house, or vegetation. This dreary place is in the North Riding of Yorkshire, and of it many a melancholy and frightful legend is told; but it is not of *Black Hammilton* I have to speak, but of the lonely hut I before mentioned, which formed a pitiful shelter to myself, two other half starved looking children younger than me, a boy and a girl; a savage black whiskered looking man, who I was taught to believe was my father, and a poor emaciated meek eyed woman, whose affectionate care of me made me love her, and who I thought at that time possessed a claim from nature on my fondest affections. The memory is ever more faithful when sharpened by sorrowful recollections, and well do I remember, the bitter misery of those years of my childhood. The place we inhabited had only two small rooms, whose walls were broken and decayed, forming but weak barriers to the winter's chilling blast, and the tempest's alarming fury. It was just one of those kind of miserable abodes which are so often described in the pages of a romance. Many a dreary day, and cheerless night do I recollect, myself and my brother and sister as I thought they were, being huddled together, round a broken hearth, on which was kindled a fire from the

furze; which we could gather on the common, while our poor mother, with looks wan with inward anguish, and haggard with want, would sit in one corner, and with eyes that were teeming with tears, would watch us with heart-rending solicitude; and with the most tender and pathetic accents seek to appease our anguish, when we cried for that food which, alas! she had not to give us!

" Those were some of the bitterest moments of my eventful life, and yet I recal them with a sort of melancholy pleasure, for with those dismal reminiscences, recurs the image of a mother, whose fondness to her offspring, no language can do ample justice to, and whose sufferings and untimely fate are sufficient to excite the deepest sympathy in the most callous breast.

" My father was generally absent all day, and frequently all night, during which times my mother never went to bed, and young as I was, I could tell by by the deep anxiety with which she watched at our cottage window, the unutterable anguish, suspense, and distraction, that were passing in her mind. As for us children, the absense of our father rather excited a feeling of gratification in our minds than any thing else, for when he was at home, the harshness of his behaviour to us, the cruelty of his conduct to our poor mother, whom he sometimes beat severely, and the general forbidding, and revolting character of his manners, were a source of the utmost terror to us; and so frightened of him had we at last become, that we used to tremble when we heard his hand upon the latch of our cottage door, and cling around our mother for protection. Sometimes we have been without food for two days together, clothes we had but a scanty allowance of, shoes and stockings were articles unknown to us; at other times our father has returned with money and watches, and jewellery of all descriptions, and then we have had a profusion of victuals, and my father would drink to excess, while my poor mother seemed more unhappy than ever, and constantly had her eyes to the door, as though she expected but feared to see some one enter."

"Then she would venture to remonstrate with my father, and to persuade him not to drink so much of the maddening liquor, but the only effect her words had upon him was, to extort a dreadful oath from him, and often a violent blow. But I am fearful I shall grow tedious by thus minutely detailing the events of my juvenility."

Here loud and simultaneous cries of "No! no!" "Proceed!" "Go on!" burst from the whole of the members of the Cadgers' Club, whose countenances told how deeply they were interested in the narrative; and Scapegrace Jack, thus encouraged, and having been prevailed upon to drink deeply out of at least a dozen different glasses, resumed his singular and soul-absorbing story, in the following words:

"Thus passed away two years, and, if it were possible, our poverty, our misery, and my father's brutality, increased; and my sister, whose young constitution was unable to fight against the privations to which we were all exposed, sank at length to the grave, and the pale cheek, squalid figure, and sunken eye, of our affectionate mother showed too distinctly the fatal ravages which penury and ill-treatment were making on her fragile frame.

"She would sit and weep over me and my brother for hours, during the lonely time of her watching, and at intervals she would cast her eyes towards Heaven, and breathe a prayer for our future welfare.

"It was on a dreadful cold night in the middle of December, when the icicles hung to every diamond of glass in the casement of our rude hovel; the snow lay like an immense shroud upon the earth, and the wind blew in hollow and moaning gusts through the numerous apertures in the walls of our hut, that my poor mother stood, as usual, watching at the casement the return of her rude partner, who had been absent from an early hour in the morning. My brother had sunk to sleep before the fire, and I sat huddled up, for the warmth, in one corner, but watching with much solicitude the behaviour of my mother. She seemed more than usually agitated, frequently sighed deeply, and then beating her breast, she would utter the name of my father, repeating at the same time a number of unconnected sentences, which I was too young to understand. Then she would walk to the door of the hut, and, opening it, walk out a few yards on to the heath beyond, and, stretching her eyes as far as she could, seemed to expect her husband's return; but she could hear nothing but the bellowing of the wind, and as the snow fell in heavy flakes upon the earth, she could not perceive any object at the distance of half a dozen yards before her. By the red glare of the fire, which cast a ghastly light upon her pale and careworn countenance, I could mark the intensity of her sufferings, and I frequently asked what she was weeping for, and why she seemed so very unhappy.

"'Nothing—nothing, my child!' she said, in a tone of deep emotion, and kissing me affectionately; 'but it is getting late—go to bed my boy—go to bed—you must be tired.'

"'Oh! no, indeed, mother,' I replied; 'I cannot sleep while you are so unhappy. Why do you cry so? Is it because we have no victuals? Oh, do not weep for that, for there is a crust of bread in the cupboard, and you can eat that, and me and Robert can go without till father comes home, who will bring us plenty, I know, although he is so cross and ill-natured to us.'

"'My poor unconscious boy!' exclaimed my mother, clasping me convulsively in her arms, and pressing her cold pale lips upon my cheek; 'but, go to rest, do, I pray you; I will soon come to you—go to rest, my child—go to rest!'

"The spirit of disobedience had not at that period of my life, found a place in my bosom; my heart was then pure and good; I had yet to experience the treachery, the cruelty, the vicissitudes of the world to make me what I afterwards became; and I did as my unfortunate parent desired me. To retire to the place we called our bed, was a task of no great difficulty! it was a miserable heap of rags in one corner of the room upon which we all of us laid, with the wretched articles of apparel with which we were so thinly clad upon us, to keep us as warm as the ruinous hovel we inhabited would allow us to be.

"'Stay, my child,' said my mother, as I was about to lay myself down, 'before you go to sleep, kneel with me, and repeat after me the prayer I utter.' With a feeling of solemnity which I cannot describe, but which even at this long distance of time is still as vivid as ever in my memory, I knelt with my mother, and after her, repeated a fervent prayer for the safety of my austere father, after which I laid myself down and pretended to endeavour to go to sleep, but sleep was entirely banished from my eyelids; I felt that something unusual was about to happen to increase our misery, and from beneath the clothes I secretly watched the actions of my mother, who paced the room with an uneasy step, ever and anon going to the casement, and then to the door, between each blast of wind listening to catch the sounds of her husbands footsteps; then she would throw herself despairingly in the chair, and wildly clasping her emaciated hands, call aloud on the name of my father, and burst into a fit of hysterical sobs, which were truly piteous to hear.

"At length completely exhausted with watching, I sunk into a disturbed slumber, but it was only to experience redoubled horrors in the most frightful dreams. I was aroused, by a distant church bell, tolling the hour of three o' clock. I looked around the room, a few embers of the fire, were still burning on the hearth, and a candle was in the window sill, which was fast dwindling into the candlestick, and from the length of the snuff, appeared to have not been attended to for some time. But where was my mother? She was not in the room; I jumped up with terror, and child as I was, felt a dreadful presentiment that something had happened to her; my little brother still slept soundly and unconscious of what had happened. With a frenzied voice I called upon the name of my mother, and when no one answered me, I wrung my hands, and raced across the room in the most dreadful anguish!

"Never shall I forget the horrors of that fatal night! Snatching up the candle, I rushed into the other room; but my mother was not there; I was alone with my brother in this wretched and lonely abode? It has often been a matter of astonishment to me, how, so young as I was, I found resolution enough to act in the manner I did on that melancholy occasion. I returned to the room below, and covering my brother up warmly with every rag I could get together, I hastily put the small portion of the candle which was left, in an old lantern, which I found in a cupboard, and with a courage unequalled at my age, I issued from the cottage door, into the wild and freezing horrors of the storm, with the hope of finding my unhappy parent.

"The snow still descended with unabated fury, and the wind came with piercing coldness to my very heart, as with my shoeless feet, I with extreme difficulty forced my way over the pathless and snow covered heath. It was a frightful place at the best of times, at night; but now it was doubly awful; nothing around to be seen but the white and ghastly snow, with here and there, the withered trunk of some old tree, which looked like some frightful spectre standing in the solemnity of the scene. I proceeded some distance, often pausing with terror, to look behind to see if any one was pursuing me, and to blow the ends of my fingers, which were quite benumbed with the intense cold! Then would I call aloud on the name of my mother, and start with terror at the awful sound of my own voice in that dismal spot! I took particular notice of the way I went, so that I might be enabled to retrace my steps to the cottage. But vain was my search; vain were my cries; I could see no traces of my unfortunate parent, and I felt myself unable to proceed farther, and with a burst of grief, such as I had never felt before, I wrung my hands, and turned slowly to make my way back to the hovel, for my candle was almost exhausted, and I knew that I should never be able to find my way home again without a light. My limbs were now stiff, and almost useless with the frost, and I felt an almost irresistable drowsiness gradually stealing over my senses, so that I was almost tempted to lay myself down on the cold and rude bed, which the snow covered earth presented to me. But I resisted the temptation. and finally reached the hovel. But oh, how shall I describe my feelings when I entered that melancholy place, and found that neither my mother or father had returned? I cried aloud in the bitterness of my anguish, and for the first time the thought occured to me, that they had both abandoned me and my brother to starvation. But in a moment after I upbraided myself for this idea, and felt convinced that some dreadful accident had befallen both my parents, or they never could have had the heart to leave us, children as we were, in this awful and desolate condition.

"My poor brother still slept peaceably, and as the embers of the fire had not yet expired, I collected what fuel I could find in the place, and kindled it into a cheerful blaze, and sitting before it, I endeavoured to restore warmth to my frozen limbs. I must pass over the torments, the unparalleled anguish, suspense and terror I suffered for the remainder of that never to be forgotten night;—sleep I could not; and I heard every quarter of an hour, chime from the church bell, till the commencement of another day, and still my parents had not returned. Oh, what a miserable day was that to me; abandoned, alone with my brother, children as we were, what was to become of us?—I knew no one in the world;—our poverty had kept friends away from us, and I had scarce seen any other faces than those of my parents, and knew only by what they had told me, that there were other beings besides ourselves in existence. In the morning my brother awoke, and cried bitterly when he found that no one was there but myself. I endeavoured to appease him as well as I could, by telling him that our mother would soon be back, and at length I partially succeeded in soothing him. He was hungry, I was the same, for it was many hours since we had tasted any food, but regardless of my own wants, for sorrow made me indifferent to them, I gave him the only crust of bread there was in the hovel, and then telling him that I should not be long, and saying that I was only going to fetch mother home,—I left the cottage, recollecting that I had heard my parents speak of the village of Thirsk, being not far off, and which I determined to find if possible, vainly hoping that I might there hear something of one if not both of my wretched parents. I succeeded at last after a laborious and miserable walk, in reaching Thirsk, where perceiving a great crowd standing round a public house, I made my way up to it, and endeavoured to learn the cause of it. It was not long ere I succeeded in doing this, for every body was busily occupied in talking of the circumstance, which had brought them together. It appeared that two men who lived in Thirsk, in crossing *Black Hambleton* that morning, the snow having been partially thawed from the earth, had discovered the body of a woman, quite dead, who had evidently lost her life in the dreadful frost and snow storm, of the previous night. I heard them describe her dress; her features; and with a scream that startled all the gossipers, exclaimed:—

'"My mother! my mother! it is my poor mother!'

"The people astonished at my words, and looking with pity on my deplorable condition, requested the landlady of the house, a motherly benevolent looking old woman, to suffer me to go into her parlour, which request she complied with, and after seeing me seated before a good fire, the eager persons who had flocked into the parlour elicited from me my simple and affecting story, and I could distinguish by their looks when I had concluded, that they imagined my awful surmises were but too true. With streaming eyes, and a bursting heart, I begged them to take me to my poor mother, but they endeavoured to console me, and informed me that the body of the woman which had been found in the snow, had been taken to the house of a charitable gentleman of the name of Hoare, who resided in a large mansion in the middle of the heath, and that if I would be calm, and endeavour to take some refreshment, they would afterwards send a person to take care of my brother, who I had left by himself in the hovel, and then they would conduct me to the house of the gentleman, to ascertain if my fears were just.

"This assurance somewhat pacified me, and I endeavoured to comply with their request, by tasting a little cordial, and a mouthful of bread and meat. This being done, a person hastened according to the direction I gave her, to see after my brother, and the kind hearted hostess having put on my feet a pair of shoes, belonging to one of her own children, accompanied me to the house of Mr. Hoare. I shall pass over the scene of affliction I was there fated to undergo, when I found that my worst surmises were realized, and that the body of the hapless woman, proved to be that of my unfortunate mother. Unable longer to endure the anxiety of watching for her husband, she had quitted our hovel in search of him, and probably overcome by her own sufferings, she had fainted on the heath, and had been frozen to death. The discovery was too much for my young mind, and I became insensible. When I recovered, I found myself lying in a clean bed, and an aged and respectable looking woman leaning affectionately over me. The apartment I was in betokened a respectability that I had never before experienced, and which to me appeared almost magni_

ficent. My first questions were to ask where I was, what had become of my brother, whether my father had returned, and if my poor mother was in the house. All these inquiries were answered in the most tender manner by the good woman who attended upon me, and I learnt that I was in the hospitable house of Mr. Hoare, who upon learning my melancholy history, had ordered my brother to be brought to his house, and every thing to be done to render us comfortable. He had also taken upon himself the expenses of the funeral of my unfortunate mother, and instituted every inquiry after my unnatural father. My brother was quickly introduced to me, and he was now cleanly attired, and looked so well and so comfortable to what I had hitherto seen him, that in the fulness of my gratitude, I breathed an innocent prayer for blessings on the head of our generous protector. Mr. Hoare was a gentleman whose countenance was the very prototype of his heart, kind, benevolent, and charitable; there are few such beings in the world, or there would be no such characters as compose this honourable society. He was a widower, and had only one son about my own age. The woman who had attended me was his housekeeper. Hearing that I was restored to sensibility, he shortly visited me, and with the most kind words endeavoured to reconcile me to my situation, and assured me that he would be a friend to me and my brother. I begged once more to be allowed to gaze upon the remains of my poor mother, but this from prudential motives he would not agree to, and I endeavoured to reconcile myself. I soon recovered my health, for the kind treatment I experienced quickly had the most fortunate effects on me, and my benefactor was pleased to assure me that if I behaved myself, he would in future become a parent to me and my brother. Although I have not the slightest doubt that he knew at that time the real fate of my father, he never told me of it, probably from an anxiety not to wound my feelings; and it was only by mere accident that I afterwards learned the miserable end of the author of my being. He had formerly been a man of considerable property, which he had entirely squandered in dissipation, and was reduced to beggary; the small remains of principle that had been left in his bosom were stifled; he turned robber, and on the night on which my mother lost her life, he was apprehended in an attempt at highway robbery, and being found guilty, forfeited his life to the offended laws of his country. My narrative has hitherto been of the most sombre description, but I shall shortly come to that period of my life which will unfold a greater variety of wonderful and humorous adventures than have ever before befallen a CADGER."

Here the learned Jack once more paused in his marvellous story, and as it was getting late, he suggested the propriety of deferring the recital of the remainder of his adventures to the following evening. After some demurring on the part of many of the members, who were impatient to hear the rest of Jack's narrative, it was finally assented to, and after several excellent songs from the members, and when the learned Mr. Jumper had persisted in performing a curious and characteristic waltz with one *Miss Dimity Bet*, (as she was elegantly named by the fraternity,) a lady of Warren complexion ; and had finally fallen under the table in his usual blissful state of sublimation, the club broke up, some of the learned members retired to their *virtuous bug walks ;* others, less fortunate, to the Piazzas, Covent Garden, and the remainder to court Morpheus on the *the twopenny rope.*

CHAP. IV.

THE MARVELLOUS ADVENTURES OF SCAPEGRACE JACK CONTINUED.—HE LOSES HIS PATRON, AND IS THROWN UPON THE WORLD.—HIS ENCOUNTER WITH THE GIPSIES.—THE GIPSIES' CAROUSAL.—THE MURDER. — THE FLIGHT. — THE JOURNEY TO LONDON.—JACK MEETS WITH TWO NEW ACQUAINTANCES. AND WHAT OCCURS TO HIM IN CONSEQUENCE. — THE BEGGAR'S HAUNT.—A LECTURE UPON CADGING, AND A DISSERTATION UPON THIEVING.

THE next night the learned Society of Cadgers assembled an hour earlier, and after the usual preliminary ceremonies had been gone through, Scapegrace Jack resumed his adventures in the following manner :—

" I shall pass hastily over three years of my life, during which I experienced the utmost kindness from my benefactor ; he educated both me and my brother, and in all respects behaved to us with the same affection as he did to his own son ; my brother, however, who was of a most delicate constitution, did not live to evince his sense of the vast obligation he was under to him, and to add to my misfortune, my kind-hearted benefactor shortly afterwards sickened and died, and thus was I deprived of the only friend who had the means and the will, to place me in a respectable situation of life ; but although at that time it was to me a source of much grief, I have ever since rejoiced in the circumstance, as had it not taken place, I should probably have been nothing more than a plain, simple, plodding merchant, or at best, a gentleman all my days, and never have experienced that delightful series of adventures which I have met with in my various characters of gipsey, beggar, crossing-sweeper, letter-writer, and general cadger. But I am detaining from you the more interesting portion of my adventures.

"After the death of my benefactor, his affairs were left to his brother, who was made the guardian of his son, and was desired in his will to continue the same protection to me that he had done, until I had arrived at the age of maturity. Whether or not the good man left me any property, I could never learn, although I doubt not he did ; however, I never received a farthing, and the first use my new guardian made of his power, was to turn me out of doors one cold night, and command me, on pain of punishment, never to presume to venture near that house again, in which I had till then, experienced so much kindness. In vain I expostulated, and begged of the old villain to take into consideration my youth, and the friendless and helpless condition I was placed in ; he only replied by calling me an impudent young beggar's brat, and ordered two of the male domestics to turn me from the door ; this they obeyed to the very letter, the door was closed in my face, and I was left upon the dreary heath, alone and friendless.

" I need not attempt to describe to you the state of my sufferings at that time ; they may better be imagined. I was then no more than ten years of age, and extremely small and delicate. The night was bitter cold, and I was upon a heath one and twenty miles in extent, destitute of a single friend, without a farthing, unacquainted with the world, and ignorant which way to direct my footsteps. For a few minutes I cried bitterly; then at last a thought occurred to me that I would endeavour to reach the public house kept by the kind hearted woman I have before mentioned in my narrative, and beg of her a lodging for the night. It was with much difficulty I put this design into execution, as the earth was frozen over and so slippery that I could scarcely keep my feet, and it was a very late hour when I reached the public house, and fortunately I found the hostess still up, as she was awaiting the return of her husband. I briefly informed her of the cause of my visit, and the cruel behaviour of my late benefactor's brother, and she listened to me with much commiseration, and afterwards made me retire to rest with her children, on the condition that I would accompany her in the morning to the house of my late protector, when she said she would herself try her influence to make my oppressor relent, assuring me at the same time that if she was unsuccessful in her praiseworthy efforts, she could render me no further assistence, as she was very poor, had a large family, and that her husband was a very harsh, and cruel sort of a man, and would probably ill-treat her, if he knew that she had even done the trifling service she was about to render me. My gratitude was unbounded, and I promised to be directed entirely by her. I passed a wretched night, for the thoughts of my miserable and forlorn condition would not suffer me to sleep, and in the morning, when the landlady's husband had gone out to his usual employment, I arose, and entering the parlour, she gave me a hearty breakfast with her own children, and then we immediately started across *Black Hambleton*, to the house of which I had so lately been an inmate. Our reception, and the result of our interview with the heartless man, I shall not particularly describe, I need only say that all the remonstrances of the good hostess, and the artless prayers and intreaties of myself, were quite unavailing, and he threatened to give us both into the tender care of Gall, the parish beadle, if we did not immediately quit the place. The landlady was much affected at the unsuccess of her designs, and a thousand times praying for my future welfare, and expressing again and again her poignant regret that she could not take me home until something had been done for my future support, she slipped a shilling into my hand, and left me."

"Thus did I enter that path, which, after a multiplicity of unparalleled adventures, finally conducted me to the enviable station I now occupy. The hostess had seen me as far as the high road, and there I seated myself on a mile-stone, and with a bursting heart, reflected what was to become of me. It may be asked, why did I not apply to the parish! But no, child as I was, I had heard too much of the bitter sufferings inflicted by the scoundrels of a parish workhouse, on the hapless children of poverty, to entertain any other feeling than that of the utmost horror and detestation of them; and I looked upon starvation even as preferable to the lingering death inflicted by the ill-treatment of what are wrongfully and inappropriately termed the *guardians* of the poor! But where was I now to turn?—What could a boy like me do alone, and unprotected in the world?—While I thus bitterly reflected, a mail coach drove past me, on which the name of London attracted my notice; a thought immediately darted across my mind.

"I had often heard my late benefactor and his friends talk about the busy metropolis, the life that was going forward there, and the various schemes that were resorted to by its inhabitants to procure a living; 'If I could only find my way there,' thought I to myself, 'surely I could meet with some means of obtaining a living!' In a moment I decided upon going to London to try my fortune, and off I started accordingly, having nothing in the world but the shilling the kind hostess had given to me. Had I had any idea of the difficulties I might have to encounter in the course of the journey, or of the distance it was to London, it is more than probable, that I should never have had the courage to have started, and thus I might never have had the opportunity of meeting with those curious adventures I am now about to detail to you; but the world to me was then all the same, and young as I was, I felt confident that it mattered but very little to what spot I directed my footsteps, so long as I was able to procure the necessaries of life. Away then I started, following the direction I had seen the coach take, and walking very briskly, until I was quite tired, and was at last compelled to sit and rest myself on a mile stone; I did not indulge myself in this very long, as I was anxious to pursue my journey, and get as far on the road before night-fall, which was rapidly approaching, as I could, and I feared to travel in the dark. Soon after this I reached a village, and being very hungry I went into a shop and bought a penny loaf, with which, and a draught of water from a neighbouring spring, I made an economical meal, and pursued my way, somewhat refreshed. As night, however, rapidly approached, I felt my spirits fail me, and began to feel more poignantly than ever the utter misery of my fate. What thought I, was to become of me?—Where could I rest? —Who would give a shelter to a poor friendless child? — What could I do when the trifle in money I had about me was exhausted?—To add to my melancholy, I had strayed from the direct road in the bewilderment of my thoughts, and found myself in the intricate mazes of a thick wood, through which the pale light of the moon could scarcely penetrate. In vain I sought to regain the path I had wandered from, it was completely lost to me, and at length worn out with fatigue and terror, I crawled into the hollow trunk of a tree, and endeavoured to compose my mind to sleep 'till the morning. This was a task of no easy accomplishment, and it was some time ere I succeeded in it, but at length completely overcome with fatigue and anxiety of mind, I dropped off into an uneasy slumber, from which I was aroused by loud shouts, laughing, and singing, which seemed to issue near me. I listened and trembled every limb of me with terror, for the voices seemed chiefly to be those of men, and occasionally a dreadful oath would meet my ears, which at that time struck the most indescribable horror to my soul. I was almost afraid to move, and for some time I durst not look from the place in which I was, so alarmed was I, at the novelty of my situation. At length, however, I did venture to peep from my lodging, and beheld at a very short distance from me, a number of large fires, kindled on the earth, round which were gathered various groups of persons, whose wild and ruffianly appearance, tattered garments, and rude countenances, were indistinctly revealed to me by the red glare of their fires. In different places, I could also distinguish small tents, which were also surrounded by a number of strange looking figures, who as well as I could see were drinking and carousing.

"A very good idea may now be formed of the terror which predominated in my breast at this sight, in a moment I concluded them to be thieves, and I trembled for the consequences should they discover me in my retreat; they would probably think that I was some spy upon their actions, and perhaps cruelly treat me, or murder me. For a moment I thought within myself, that my safest plan would be to take to immediate flight; but then again I reflected that that would be only madness as I was so unacquainted with the mazes of the forest, and in endeavouring to escape might probably throw myself into the power of the wretches I wished to avoid.

I therefore determined to stay where I was, and leave my fate in the hands of Providence. For more than an hour, I could hear the rude and boisterous revelry of the persons who had so much alarmed me, and frequently a line or so of the wild songs they were singing would vibrate on my ear, aud from the nature of which I had too much reason to fear that my worst surmises as regarded their characters were true. Suddenly by the glare of their fires, I could perceive a stir among them; the voices of joviality ceased; and I could discover a number of coarsely clad beings quitting the scene of their late carousal, and moving in the same direction as where I was secreted.

"What a state of painful anxiety and consternation was I now in; at first I half issued from my place of conceal-ment, and intended to take to flight, but recollecting that the robbers might have dispersed themselves in various parts of the wood, and that I might fall into their hands, I thought it safer to remain where I was, where I at least had a chance of safety. I pinched myself up to the smallest possible compass, and almost feared to breathe, more especially as I could distinctly hear the robbers, as I surmised them to be, approaching the very tree which formed my hiding place. They had now got so near to me that I could distinctly hear every word they uttered, and overheard the follow-ing not remarkably interesting conver-sation.

"'I don't half like this business to-night,' said a coarse voice, 'I'm afraid there will be something wrong in the *crack*, for in the first instance the *kid's* a size too large or more I know to make a safe *dodge* into that small window.'

"'It's a pity the gipseying bus'ness falls off so;' returned another voice which seemed to be that of an old man, 'I can remember the time when we had no occasion to turn housebreakers to get a living, and except in the shape of a little plate which we occasionally *found* at a gentleman's house when we went to tell the servant girls their fortunes, or some tender poultry which we *borrowed* from the farm houses, there was not a more honest profession in the world than a gipsey.'

"'Ah, times are very much altered Michael,' said the first voice, 'but it's no fault of ours that we turn dishonest; if ladies will get so silly as not to have their fortunes told, and if gentlemen will be so stingy as to refuse to relieve our wants, who's to blame I should like to know?—They can't expect that *we* can put up with the loss you know. It was a bad job our losing that young scamp Gilbert, the other day, he was a natty little figure, and just the right size for our business; it must have been that affair with the—.'

"'Hush!' interrupted the other voice, 'that was indeed a cruel affair, and I think I shall never forget it as long as I live!—How the poor old man prayed for mercy; and when the red blood streamed from that ghastly wound in his head, and stained his silvery locks, I thought—'

"'Damn what you thought!' exclaimed the course and disagreable voice of the first person who had spoken, 'you are continually prating about that old miser. I think there was great credit due to me for the manner in which I managed that business, and made him reveal the place in which he had concealed his treasure, It was a deep trick of the old fellow to hide it in the trunk of a tree, but I was one too many for him; I say, Mike, why I'm d—d if this a'n't the very tree; come here, and I'll show you the artful manner in which the old fellow had concealed his gold!'

"You may readily conceive," continued Scapegrace Jack, addressing himself to his attentive and deeply interested auditors, "you may readily conceive the sensation of horror which crept through my veins while this discourse was going on; it was sufficient to inform me that the fellows were of the very worst description of characters, and that their trade and traffic was robbery and murder; but intense as those emotions were, they were nothing compared to those which took possession of me when I found that the very tree to which the

ruffian alluded in his discourse, was the tree in which I was at present concealed, and moreover that he was approaching it for the very purpose of shewing his companion the place in which their unfortunate victim had concealed his treasure. I now of course gave myself up for lost, and my first impulse was to issue from my place of concealment, and throwing myself on my knees before the rude and meanly clad wretches before me, I called aloud for their pity and mercy!—

"'Ah, a spy! a spy!' shouted several voices at once, as the light faintly emitted from a dark lantern which they carried with them, darted across my pallid and horror-stricken countenance.

"'Kill him! murder him!' exclaimed two or three savage voices, and in a moment I felt my arm grasped fiercely, and two or three long knives were held to my throat, and a pistol was leveled to my head! I screamed with perfect and indescribable horror, and again I prayed for mercy.

"'Hold!' cried one of the ruffians, in whom I recognised the man who had been addressing the conversation to Michael, thrusting the hands of his comrades from me, and pulling me violently on my feet; 'Speak, youngster, what brings you here, and what are you?—No falsehoods, you know, for I am sure to detect you, and will immediately scatter your brains upon the earth if you attempt to deceive me!'

"In a voice which betrayed the extreme terror under which I laboured, I gave the villian as brief and as correct an account of myself, as my memory would allow me. The gipsies all listened to me with attention, and when I had concluded my simple story, the fellow who had commanded me to relate it, seemed to eye me with suspicion, and irresolution, and after a pause of a minute or two; he suddenly ejaculated;—

"'Did you hear the conversation which lately passed between me and one of my comrades?—Answer truly, boy, for on it your life depends!'

"I shuddered with horror at this question, but I thought it would be better to tell the truth than to seek to hide it; I repeated every sentence I had heard them utter. No sooner had I concluded, than several of the villians again demanded my life, declaring that I had heard too much for them to suffer me to live; that their own safety demanded that I should be murdered. This would no doubt soon have been put into execution, had it not been for the interposition of the ruffian of whom I have before spoken, and who seemed to have some authority over the rest, who commanded them to desist, and taking them aside, he whispered to them for a few minutes, often pointing towards me, and seeming to direct their attention to my youth, and the delicacy of my figure. While this consultation was going forward, my mind was in the most horrible state of suspense that can be conceived; but at length, they seemed to have come to some satisfactory conclusion, for the before mentioned ruffian approaching me, took my hand and drawing me into the midst of his ferocious looking companions, he looked sternly into my countenance for a few seconds, and then addressed me in the following strain :—

" ' Boy, accident has thrown you into the hands of those, who were they probably sufficiently mindful of their own safety, would immediately put you beyond the power of betraying them; but your youth and the tale you have told us of your misfortunes, have induced us to treat you with mercy. Your life is safe on one condition, which is that you keep a secret in your own breast all that you have this night heard and seen. You must never again quit our tribe, and so you had best endeavour to conciliate our good opinion, by seeking to render yourself useful, in whatever we may think proper to set you to do, than by any act of disobedience incur that severe punishment we shall never fail to inflict. From this hour you must be one of us; you must do as we do, and a merry and happy life you'll have of it.'

"Oh, how I shuddered with horror, while the gipsey was giving utterance to this speech; but I sought to stifle my emotions, and to resign myself to my fate, seeing how fruitless it would be for me to attempt any thing like an expostulation against it.

" ' Do you know the meaning of an oath, boy ?' inquired the ruffian, after a pause, during which he been stedfastly contemplating my countenance. I answered in the affirmative, and he administered to me an oath to keep secret every transaction I might in future see done in the gang to which he belonged, and also to keep faithful to them in whatever situation I might be placed. With trembling lips I took the required oath, although of course in my heart I revolted from it, and considered that no vow extorted from a person by intimidation could be binding.

" ' All right, my fine fellow,' said the gipsey, when I had complied with his request, ' I shall soon find you something to do, never fear. I say, Michael, what do you think of him ? don't you think he'll be a very good substitute for that young runaway Gilbert ?—See what limbs he's got; why a spider might quarrel with him for robbing him of his gentility.'

" ' The kinchin's well enough for the make of him;' replied the hoary headed old wretch to whom this important question had been addressed, ' but its the pluck you know; there's not many *men* who are so game as that devil's bastard, Gilbert was.

" ' If game is all he wants,' exclaimed the other, ' we shall soon instil that into him, never fear; and so the sooner we begin with him the better. Suppose we give him a trial in the present *crack*, and in order that we may give him a few instructions, and introduce him to our comrades, I think we had better delay the job until to-morrow night.'

" To this proposition the others all agreed, and the villains drove me before them towards the fires that were still burning before their tents. Having got there, I beheld a number of gipsey women, some of them of the most savage appearance, and some young girls whose large black eyes and nut-brown countenances had a very striking and interesting effect. They were most of them occupied in cooking some viands in large iron pots suspended over the fires, while others were lolling on pieces of canvass spread upon the earth, while here and there a ragged looking man was seated upon a rude block made rut of the piece of a trunk of a tree, smoking a short and blackened pipe, and looking with an air of indifference on all around him. There were three tents, in one of which the whole of the gang reposed, and the earth was strewn with the hides of sheep, which served for the gipsies bed.

"The gipsies eyed me with no very agreeable or prepossessing looks, but when I had been introduced to them, and another consultation had been carried on in whispers among them, they looked upon me with something like kindness, and one of the women telling me to warm myself by the fire, asked me if I was hungry? My heart was too full to suffer me to appease the cravings of hunger, and I replied that I was not in want of any thing. The remainder of the gang shortly after returned, bringing with them sheep, pigs, and poultry, which they had killed, and taken from some farmers who had refused to relieve them, and who resided at the other side of the forest. They seemed not a little astonished when they beheld me among them, but that surprise was quickly done away with when *Alec the Badger*, as I learnt the gipsey of whom I have so often spoken, was called, described the manner in which they had found me, and what he had done, and the objects he had in view as regarded me, and they seemed all of them to feel perfectly satisfied with what Alec had done. After passing various opinions upon my personal appearance, and of the uses for which they should probably be able to qualify me, which to me were any thing but satisfactory; they ordered the women to bring forward their repast, which was quickly done, and presented a plenteous supply of viands, which showed that the gipsies love of good living was one of the most prominent features of their character. In spite of the state of my mind, they compelled me to eat, and I did so, fearful of what might be the dreadful consequences of my disobedience.

"This meal having been despatched, the gang sat down to drink, smoke, and talk over their exploits; and the crimes that they thus revealed, made me shudder at the bare idea of being in the company of such wretches. The women were not behind hand in boasting of their dishonest practices, and they indulged in many pleasant stories of the silly dupes they had made among the credulous and superstitious. One aged woman displayed a set of silver teaspoons, which she said she had *sneaked* out of a gentleman's house in the morning, to which she had gained access on the pretext of telling the servant's fortunes. And another woman who had two dirty and half naked children, shewed a silver fork, which she had induced a female servant to purloin from her master, by promising her a husband with plenty of money. All these stories of the exploits of those well-practised thieves, were received by the whole of the gang with the warmest marks of approbation, and the conversation then turned to the business they had in view for the following night, and in which it seemed they had determined that I should sustain an important character; but their language was so overwhelmed with flash phrases, that at that time I was totally at a loss to understand their meaning.

"'Mat,' exclaimed Alec, addressing himself to a lad about fourteen years old, who was lazily stretching his half naked limbs before the fire, and smoking a short pipe with as much ease and apparent enjoyment, as the oldest among the company;—'Mat, you must try the *dodge* in some other way now for the benefit of the gang; we sha'n't want your services now in the *crack* department, as we've got this youngster;—it's a lucky job for us that we have picked him up, for you lead such a lazy life that you've got too fat for any thing now, and I don't know how we should have got over, that business to morrow night with you.'

"The lad to whom this was spoken was an abridged edition of the Newgate Calendar;—he had small pigish looking eyes, which ever and anon glared artfully from beneath a copious pair of black eye-brows; his hair was long and ragged; his cheek bones high, his forehead low, and the darkness of his complexion which was that of a Greek, was a sufficient evidence of his gipsey origin.

He seemed to treat the observations of *Alec the badger*, with much indifferance, and turned upon me a look which was one of the most disagreeable I had ever beheld.

"'Well, it can't be helped;' replied this interesting youth, evacuating a thick volume of smoke, and spitting betwixt his teeth; 'I must see what I can do upon the *"mace,"* that's all!—Besides, you know I only took th' office to oblige you, arter the loss o' young Gilbert.'

"'True,' replied Alec, 'and I must say you have done as well as was in your power. But that will be a very awkward job. Zarah went to the house this morning, and she took a good survey of it, and she says that the glaze is hardly large enough to let a cat through.'

"'And it's very high in the wall too,' observed another of the gipsies, 'and if the young 'un should not be able to climb——'

"'Oh, that will be right enough,' interrupted Alec, 'we can easily give him a lift up, and when he's once through the window, he can descend on the other side easy enough, for there is a lot of old lumber piled against the wall.'

"'But how will you manage about the dog?' inquired another of the gang.

"'Oh, Zarah, is going to the house to morrow,' answered Alec, 'to tell the old cook her fortune, and she can easily sneak into the yard, and give the dog a dose that will stop his barking before night comes, I'll warrant!'

"'Who's to be in the business?' asked the gipsey.

"'Why, I think *the wolf* and myself will be quite enough,' replied Alec, 'the other's had better be striking the tents, and getting every thing ready for us to make ourselves scarce, for if we are seen on this spot an hour only after the job is done, it's a chance if some of us don't swing on the tree that bears no leaves for it!'

"'Right!' coincided all the gipsies, and it was then proposed that they should retire to rest.

"'What will you do with the Kid?' inquired Michael.

"'Oh, he can sleep by the side of me,' answered Alec, 'and then I can see after his safety. Gordon, it is your turn to keep watch. Come along youngster, and hark ye, see if you can't twist that face of yours into something more courageous, by to morrow, for you will have more to do than you think for.'

"Seeing that I was too bewildered and frightened, to comply immediately with his commands, Alec roughly grasped my arm and followed by the rest of the gipsies, led me to the tents where they slept. Men, women, and children, all reposed together, and *the badger* having first desired me to lay down in my clothes in one corner of the tent, placed his pistols above his head, and laid down by the side of me, Gordon keeping watch outside the tents.

"The villanous occupants of the sleeping tent were soon all fast locked in the arms of Morpheus, and I was left to the indulgence of my own melancholy reflections. Even at this distance of time, the recollection of what mental anguish I endured on that night is as vivid in my memory as if it had taken place but yesterday. The conversation of the fellows convinced me that their designs for the following night were housebreaking, and that they had determined I should act no unimportant part in it. but of what that part was to be, I could form not the slightest conception; that my ruin was resolved upon I was perfectly convinced, and what could I, a child, offer in opposition to it?— I was completely lost and a thousand times upbraided myself for having been so careless as to miss the right road, and to become lost in the intricacies of the wood. What would I not have given if I had had it, to have had the means of escape? but that was quite hopeless. Gordon, who guarded without the tents, presented an insurmountable obstacle, and I gave myself up to the most unutterable despair.

"After a night of the most dreadful anxiety, I arose in the morning, pale, ill, and spiritless. *The badger* and a portion of the gang went out as soon as we had partaken of a coarse but plenteous meal, and left me to the sole care and instructions of *the wolf*, as the ruffian who was to take a share in the nefarious proceedings of the night was not inappropriately designated by the gang.

"*The wolf* was a man whose very countenance struck a thrill of horror to my bosom. He was a man with a hard set of features, such as bespoke him to be of the greatest determination and reckless ferocity. He was apparently about fifty years of age, with a countenance swarthy, and very much seamed and disfigured with the ravages of the small-pox. His hair was black as jet, and hung in links down his cheeks. His eyes were small, and deep set in his head; his cheek-bones were high, and his forehead was low and contracted. His chin betokened that the luxury of a razor was seldom indulged in by him, and there was a constant wicked grin around his huge mouth, which conveyed a feeling to the heart of the beholder, of the utmost disgust. He was attired in a large rough dirty white top coat, ragged trowsers, a peculiar pair of flash-looking boots, and a hat of the most mis-shapen and inelegant description surmounted his head.

"For some minutes after the departure of *the badger* and the rest of the gang, which included the whole of the women, *the wolf* and Mat sat by the fire, smoking most vigorously at short black pipes, and ever and anon eyeing me with glances that made me tremble.

"'Mat,' at length ejaculated *the wolf*, in a hoarse tone of voice, and emitting a large cloud of smoke from his mouth, ' I dare say now you are summut down in the muns at being out o' this job to-night.'

"Mat replied by a silent bend of the head, and seemed to endeavour to bury his regret in the hearty whiffs he took at his pipe.

"' I fancy it will be a good spec,' resumed *the wolf*, 'the old buffer's as warm as a gold mine, and has al'us a good sum at home. A werry sensible and considerate thing that, o' these here rich old blades, keeping dumps in their coffers, or I don't know vot vould become o' us kids!'

"'Werry,' laconically coincided Mat.

"'That's no bad 'un for a scheme, that same Mother Zarah,' continued the robber, 'see how nicely she walked round th' servants of the house, and got out on 'em vhere the old boy kept his ochre.'

"'Ah, leave old Zarah alone for a job o' th' kind,' said Mat, ''th' gang couldn't do werry vell vithout her. But are yer sure the *spell* is made all *slap?*'

"'Clear as a finger post,' answered *the wolf*, 'there is a back door which is never fastened, the kinchin can easily get into the hall, and open the front door to me an' *th' badger*. Th' old kid sleeps in the third room opening into the gallery up the first flight o' stairs in the left ving; none o' th' servants snooze near him, for the other rooms is not habited in that ving, and th' old boy prefars it acause on its loneliness. The jimmy vill soon open the old boy's bedroom door, and then the bis'ness vill be done in a jiffy.'

"'But if he should vake, and raise any alarm;' suggested Mat.

"*The wolf* received this idea with a look which was perfectly demoniacal; and after feeling in one of his side pockets for a second or so, he drew forth a large clasp knife, and opening the blade, passed it significantly backwards and forwards within the eighth of an inch of his throat, as he replied:—

"'Vy, if he does, this yer know—' He did not finish the sentence, for Mat seemed thoroughly to comprehend his meaning, and nodded his head in token of his approval.

"Oh, how my heart shuddered while this awful conversation was going on, and I could not stifle an involuntary shriek when I saw the wretch passing the knife across his throat, and could not for a moment misconceive the meaning he intended to imply. The wretch observed my terror, and looked upon me with a savage grin, as he cried:—

"'What are you screaming at, fool?'

"'I—I—I—did not scream, sir,' I stammered forth, scarcely knowing what I uttered.

"'It's a lie!' replied *the wolf*, with all the fierceness of his name-sake. 'Why you look as white as a boiled turnip;—Come here!'

"I am ve—very well where I am, sir," I replied, shrinking back with horror from the villain's touch.

"'Come here, I say, you damned fool!' exclaimed *the wolf*, grasping my arm with a violence that made me writhe with agony, and forcibly dragging me towards him.

"'Look here, brat,' he continued, holding up the knife close to my vision, 'do you know what this is?'

"It is a knife," I answered, in a voice scarcely audible, and trembling more violently than before, for at that moment a dreadful thought occurred to me, that that the ruffian was actually going to murder me.

"'Oh, a knife is it?' returned he, after a frightful scowl, which was warmly participated in by the juvenile villain who was his companion. 'Well, and did you never see a knife afore?'

"In a timid tone I replied in the affirmative.

"'Well then, you young spoon,' cried *the wolf*, 'what made you so squeamish vhen you seed it just now.'

"I scarcely knew what answer to make to this question, but at length with tears in my eyes, I begged the wretch to forgive me if I had offended him; upon which appeal, himself and Mat indulged in a very loud fit of laughter, and cracked various jokes upon the softness of my head, the chicken quality of my heart, and various other little inuendos, which in their estimations seemed to savour of the very quintessence of wit. This exuberance of mirth having lasted for a minute or two, *the wolf* once more put his hands into each of his coat pockets, and at length brought forth to view two pistols as I too soon learnt they were, although at that time I was quite ignorant of their uses or their names.

"'Do you know vot these here is?' said he, winking significantly at Mat at the same time.

"I replied in the negative.

"'Oh, yer don't, eh?' repeated *the wolf*.

"I reiterated the negative.

"'Come here, then;' he added, drawing me closer towards him, 'I'll teach yer; and at the same instant he fired one off close to my ear, and stunned and alarmed, I sank upon the earth, while the ruffian and his companion gave way to a second fit of laughter of much more extravagance than the former one.

"'Get up yer milksop!' cried *the wolf*, dragging me on to my feet, 'vell, I never seed sich a rank cur in all my born days!'

"'If he comes that here to night,' remarked Mat, 'he'll make a nice mess on it!'

"'He'd better not!' exclaimed *the wolf*, eyeing me with a dreadful aspect, 'by hell, if he does— but come here, boy!'

"I was still stupified with the noise the report of the pistol had made, and could scarcely recollect where I was; but *the wolf* unmindful of my agitation, drew me to the other side of the tent, and pointed out to me a hole in the canvass which the bullet had perforated.

"'You see that hole!' he said.

"I stammered out 'yes.'

"'Well then, fancy that you have disobeyed me, and that you had been standing where that canvass is, that hole would have been made in your skull, and I'll be bound would have taught you better manners in future!'

"My terror now completely overcoming me, I fell on my knees before the hardened ruffian, and implored him to have mercy on a poor, friendless boy, and that I would never disobey him.

"'You'd better not,' answered the wretch, 'for as sure as you do, I'll scatter your brains upon the earth!'

"This frightful speech more alarmed me than ever, but I endeavoured as much as I could to vanquish my terrors, seeing that it would only exasperate the wretches in whose power I was unfortunately thrown to treat me more cruelly.

"'Mat,' exclaimed *the wolf*, after a pause during which he had replaced the pistols in his coat pocket, 'suppose we have a horn or two of the inwigerati'n, th' day is werry cold, and our comrades vill not return for some time to come, so I don't see vhy ve shouldn't enjoy ourselves.'

"'To be sure,' said the hopeful Mat. And with that he went to a chest which stood in one corner of the tent, and took out a bottle, and a couple of horns, extracted the cork, and filling both the horns, handed one to *the wolf* and retained the other himself.

"'Here's success to th' crack to night!' said *the wolf*, which same toast Mat reiterated, and they both swallowed the beverage which the horns contained, with much apparent relish.

"'That's a drop o' th' right sort,' said Mat, smacking his lips, 'some o' that ve got from old Jackson th' smuggler!'

"'Ah! it's werry good;' exclaimed *the wolf*, 'Mat, fill us another horn.'

"With this request, Mat complied with much avidity, doing the same favour of course for himself, and the two villains swallowed two more horns full of the beverage which seemed so agreeable to their palates, with extraordinary expedition.

"All this time I had seated myself as far from them as I conveniently could, but, *the wolf*, and Mat having resumed their pipes, the former turned to me, and with his usual stern look and voice exclaimed :—

"'Come here, young chicken heart!'

"With a faltering step I advanced.

"'Sit down there!' said *the wolf*, pointing to a hamper which was placed betwixt himself and Mat. I obeyed, and the gipsey fixed his savage eyes upon my countenance, and seemed to examine every lineament of my features and person with much intensity, keeping a profound silence for a few minutes.

"'Vhat's yer name, young 'un?' at length he inquired.

"'John, sir, I replied meekly.

"'Vell, Jack,' returned *the wolf*, 'who do yer belong to, and vot brought yer vhere ve found yer?—I s'pose you've cut yer lucky out o' some *vool-hole*.'

"At that time not understanding the latter name which he applied to the workhouse, I proceeded in a fearful and simple manner, to relate my melancholy history to them. They paid much attention to it, but I did not see that it excited their commiseration, the portion of my narrative which seemed to particularly interest them was that which related to my father, and when I mentioned the manner in which we lived, and the circumstance of my father's mysterious disappearance, a thought seemed to strik *the wolf*; and he interrupted me hastily by saying :—

"'Vot is yer name, boy, besides Jack?'

"Redgar, sir?" replied I.

———

CADGERS' CLUB.

"'Vell, who'd a thought it,' exclaimed *the wolf* taking the pipe from his mouth for a minute, and placing both hands upon his knees, he stared at me with more curiosity than ever; 'And are you the brat o' poor Jack Redgar?—Mat,' continued he turning to that named individual, 'Mat, poor Jack Redgar the father o' this here kid, vos vun o' th' finest cracksmen, and road padders that ever handled a jimmy or a barker!—He and I used to be old pals afore I joined this here gang, an' many a good svag ve have made together; I vos vith him the werry night vot finished his b's'ness!— Ve had planned it to lay vait for an old farmer that Jack knowed, and who had

been to Barnsley in the day to take a deal o' money, Jack knew th' road he alvas travelled, an' so ve remained on th' look out for him.

"'Ve had not been there long before ve saw the farmer approaching toward us, riding steadily on an old grey mare, an' out ve pops upon him. The old buffer shewed pluck though, an' resisted. I vos for silencing him directly, and it had been vell for Jack if he had been o' th' same mind; but somehow or other he turned chicken-hearted, an' vould neither use his own barker, nor suffer me to make use o' mine. Vell th' old farmer still resisted, and fought like a devil; hows'ever ve floored him, an' should werry soon ha' had his dust, vhen as ill luck vould have it, just at that moment about half a dozen peeple came up to the spot. 'Fly, fly, Jack,' said I, popping off my barker, and bringing vun o' the lot as quiet as possible to the earth. Hows'ver poor Jack vos too much confused to do as I told him; I made my lucky all right, but Jack vos nailed, and he danced th' cracksman's valtz for it too!—Yes, Jack,' continued *the wolf*, addressing himself to me, 'your father vos as good a man as ever vos *topped*!'

"Although this dreadful recital had been couched in language not altogether intelligent to me at that time, yet I could too well understand the awful fate to which my unfortunate but guilty father had brought himself, and my feelings were so overpowered that I wept aloud.

" 'Vhy, did yer ever see sich a vater pot in all yer life?' exclaimed the *wolf* to Mat, 'vot are yer slobberin' for?— Your father is not the fust man vot ever vos *topped*; I'm afeard you'll never arrive at that there *honner*, unless you profits by my instructions; if yer does that, by the help o' good luck, I may make yer as fine a feller as yer father!'

"I made a desperate effort to stifle my emotions, seeing the displeasure with which the savage ruffian eyed me, and fearful of the desperate extremities to which his exasperation might lead him.

" 'Mat,' ejaculated *the wolf*, after another pause, in which he had been puffing forth the tobacco-smoke with much rapidity, apparently indulging in the reminiscences of the past days of his glory, 'give us another drop out of the bottle; ve must drink to th' mem'ry o' poor Jack Redgar!'

" 'To be sure ve vill,' said Mat, and immediately both horns were refilled, and the two gipsies drank to the memory of my unfortunate parent.

" 'Now fill th' kinchin a horn, it vill do him good!' said *the wolf*. Mat proceeded to do as he was told, and filling a horn up to the very brim, he handed it to *the wolf*, who turned to me and said :—

" 'Now, boy, drink this off, to th' mem'ry o' yer father, and vish as how yer may some day or other turn out as bright a man as he did! Come, no flinching, swallow it down.'

" With a trembling hand I took the horn, which contained Hollands, and put it towards my lips, but the sickly fumes which arose from the intoxicating liquor was too much for my youthful stomach, my heart heaved at it, and, taking it away from my mouth in utter disgust, I exclaimed :—

" 'Indeed—indeed, sir, I—I cannot—I cannot!'

" 'Yer can't!' exclaimed *the wolf*, with increasing sternness, 'yer'd better say yer von't.'

" 'Oh! no, sir!' I replied in a piteous tone, 'indeed I do not wish to seem obstinate, but I—I cannot drink that nasty stuff.'

" 'But I tell yer yer shall, young hell-dog,' vociferated *the wolf* fiercely, and thrusting the hateful horn back to my lips; 'yer know vot I told yer about disobedience? Do yer vant to be reminded in this here vay?' And with these words the wretch put his hand into his coat pocket, and presented the pistol once more to my view. This was sufficient to frighten me into obedience, and, with a desperate effort, I swallowed the whole of the contents of the horn. I have but a confused recollection of what occurred afterwards; I have some slight remembrance of Mat refilling my glass, then the tent seemed to reel round with me, the figures of the gipsies appeared to melt into shadows before my eyes; their loud laughter became less audible in my ears, and I became insensible to every thing around me."

Just at this most interesting part of Scapegrace Jack's eventful and very romantic history he paused, for the lateness of the hour told him that it was time to leave off, as it would be impossible to come to the termination of it that night; and after some very sage observations upon what they had already heard, from several of the most learned of the members, and some remarkable and critical strictures from the renowned Mr. Jumper, the society broke up.

The adventures of Scapegrace Jack had excited a most extraordinary sensation among the cadgers, an interest that could not have been surpassed even by the relation of the far-famed *Arabian Nights*, and we have not the slightest doubt but that a feeling of a reciprocal nature already exists in the bosoms of our readers, and that they know how to appreciate the invaluable documents we have been at such infinite labour to present to them.

At an early hour on the following evening the *Cadgers' Snuggery* was again crowded by its members, and in due time Scapegrace Jack resumed his adventures in the following words :—

" When I recovered my senses, I found myself reposing in the sleeping tent, and from the noise in the adjoining tent, I could hear that the whole of the gipsies had returned, and were carousing. My head ached dreadfully, and I felt very ill. There was a light burning in the tent, and a bell at that moment chiming the hour of eleven, I found that I must have been asleep for many hours. The lateness of the hour gave me a hope that the gipsies had either abandoned their villanous design for this night, or had come to a determination to excuse me from being one of the party; but I was very soon undeceived. The singing of the gipsies suddenly ceased, and I heard a voice, which I distinguished to be that of *the badger*, say :—

" ' Come, my boy, we must be on the move; it is past eleven o'clock, and we cannot get there in less time than two hours, if we go the nearest way, which will not be very safe. Go and arouse the boy.'

" ' Ay, ay,' replied the coarse voice of *the wolf*, and the next moment I heard his heavy footfalls approaching the tent where I was. Oh, how my heart sunk at that moment; but I knew it would be useless to resist my fate, and to attempt to excite the pity of those who had no such article in their compositions, would be equally useless; I therefore hastily committed myself to the protection of Providence, and became as composed as could well be expected.

" *The wolf*, having entered the tent, approached the spot where I was lying, and not perceiving that I was awake, he pulled me roughly by the arm and

exclaimed :—' Jack, Jack! come, wake! get up, I vant yer !'

" I pretended to be awoke out of my sleep, and not to understand what he had said to me ; for I was fearful that if he thought I had been awake, he might imagine I had either been listening to the conversation of the gang, or meditating an escape.

" ' Come, don't lay there, rubbin' yer blinkers,' said the ruffian, pulling me forcibly on to my feet: ' you will have something else to do than to sleep tonight, I can tell yer. Come along !'

" He now led me into the tent in which his companions were assembled, and the gang all eyed me with much curiosity.

" ' D'ye think the kid will be all right?' asked *the badger*, addressing himself to the villain who was to be his companion in the nefarious transactions of the night.

" ' He had better,' replied *the wolf*, with one of his most disagreeabl looks; ' he knows th' consequence if he don't, that's all. But vhere's your great coat, Mat ? You can lend it to the young'un for to-night, for it is werry cold; and another thing, it may serve to disguise him in case th' traps is arter us, vhich, hows'ever. is not werry likely.'

" Mat pulled a rough white top coat from the hamper on which I had been seated in the day-time, and which fitted me something about as well as a Newfoundland dog's hide would fit a kitten, and a rough, dirty red *comforter* being twisted round my mouth, I was considered to be suitably equipped for the expedition we were going upon.

" While I was being attired by that hopeful youth Mat, the *badger* and his ferocious companions had not been unmindful of themselves, and had enveloped their persons in large top coats of the same coarse materials of which mine was made, also environing their throats in large shawls. Having done this they looked towards Mat, with an expression of countenance, which hinted to him that he had forgotten to supply them with something that was indispensably necessary for their business. As that *worthy* lad, however, did not seem perfectly to comprehend their meaning, a look of displeasure and impatience became depicted in the countenance of *the wolf* as he cried:

"'Why, vot d'yer stand there for like a fool, Mat?—Damme, if you ar'n't as green as this here kinchin!—I begin to think as how you're dipped your beak a small bit too far in that here Hollands this here arternoon!'

"'No, I've not,' sulkily replied Mat, 'but I knows werry vell who has!'

"'No more o' yer nonsense, young gallows bird!' exclaimed *the wolf*, 'vy don't yer bring the tools?—D'ye think ve can manage b's'ness vithout th' impl'ments?'

"'Oh!' laconically replied Mat, as he retired from the tent, and presently returned with a couple of black masks, two broad belts, to which were affixed by a hook, what I afterwards learned were *jemmies*, a dark lantern, a tinder-box, and matches!—These interesting looking tools he gave to *the badger* and his companion, who affixed the belts round their waists under their great coats, and placed the masks, the lantern, the tinder-box and the matches in their pockets. 'Vell, now have yer got all yer vant?' sulkily asked Mat.

"'Vhy, no!' replied *the wolf*, 'vhere the devil's th' *barkers*?'

"Mat once more retired and shortly returned with a couple of braces of large horse pistols, which the robbers also affixed in their belts, and then buttoned up their great coats close to their chins.

"'Well, we're all ready now, ain't we?' inquired *the badger*

"'Yes!' answered his comrade.

"'Very well, then, keep a tight hold of the boy's hand, and let us be off, it is getting very late, and if we don't mind we shall have the daylight peeping in upon us, long before the job is half done. Mind, boy, what I tell you, this is the last time I shall take the trouble of warning you; act in every thing as we direct you, and above all venture not to utter a word on the road, unless we ask you a question, for as sure as you do not attend to these instructions, that very moment will be the signal for us to plunge our knives to your heart!'

"I could scarcely support my weak and childish frame, during the whole of this frightful speech, but dreading the consequences of my shewing the least refractory spirit towards those in whose power I had haplessly fallen, I mustered up all my resolution, and replied in a more composed manner than could have been expected, that I would be careful and follow their advice to the best of my power.

"'Vell said, Jack!' observed *the wolf*, with an approving smile, which was as disgusting as his anger, 'only do as ve tells yer, and blest if ve sha'n't make a man of yer in no time votsumdever!'

"'There, come along!' said *the badger* in an impatient tone of voice; and followed by the good wishes of the whole of the gang for the success of our adventure, we issued from the tent into the open air.

"The night was extremely dark, and most piercingly cold, and ever and anon the wind which came in fitful gusts, whistled among the leafless trees, with that dismal and hollow sound, which to the timid ear, appears like the awful voices of some troubled spirits, or of mortals in their last extremity. Large black, and mountainous-like clouds, seemed to hang upon the summits of the trees, and not a star was visible, to give even a trifling cheerfulness to the prospect. I looked timidly around me almost every minute, with childish fear, fancying in each trunk of a tree that I approached, the alarming figure of some frightful spectre, and imagining in the blasts of the wind the voices of men.

"The two ruffians held no sort of conversation together for a great portion of the way, and they walked at the very top of their speed seeming to select the most dismal and unfrequented avenues. This precaution on their parts seemed to have been very well conceived, for not an individual did we meet until we issued from the forest, when a labouring man crossed our path, and after taking but a very slight glance at the figures of my companions, wished them good morning,' and walked on.

"*The wolf* reiterated this compliment in a feigned tone of voice, and we walked on with redoubled speed. When the countryman addressed *the wolf*, I felt that villain grasp my arm more vehe-

mently than ever; but I needed no caution of this kind, for I had quite given myself up to despair, and entertained not the slightest idea of making my escape. We walked on in the same silent and rapid manner up a long dark lane, which brought us on to a common. This common we crossed short at the right hand corner, and made our way into a narrow and unfrequented road, shaded on each side by the huge trunks of trees, which looked like an army of giants. I now heard a disant bell chime half-past one, and *the wolf* for the first time broke the silence himself and *the badger* had maintained towards each other on their journey.

" ' Half-past vun, by G——— !' he exclaimed.

" ' And it's full half an hour's walk now,' replied *the badger*, ' we must walk a little faster. Come, boy, step out, your mustn't go to sleep now, pull him along, *wolf !*'

" *Wolf* implicitly complied with this request, and increased his speed to such a degree, that I was compelled to run by his side to keep up with him. After twenty minutes hard walking, we gained the extremity of this road, and found ourselves in a small village, which was enveloped in darkness and silence as though the inmates of the humble cottages were all dead. A small wooden bridge at the top of this village brought us to a field, which we crossed in a short time, and found ourselves immediately in front of a large stone house, surrounded by a high wall, and backed by a garden.

" ' All, right, *badger*; said *the wolf*, in an under tone to his companion, ' ve are here at last !'

" ' Hush !' whispered *the badger*, ' let us take a survey !'

" I trembled more violently than I had hitherto done, when I found that the worst of my surmises as to the intentions of the two ruffians were verified; and *the wolf* muttered an oath between his teeth, and pinched my arm fiercely that I could scarcely repress a shriek.

" We walked round to the back of the house, but all was enveloped in darkness, and the wretches having listened a minute or two to hear if any thing was stiring, seemed quite satisfied.

" ' All right !' whispered *the badger* as he mounted the top of the wall with much agility.

" ' Now hand up the boy !' said he, and I was lifted up and seized in the arms of *the badger* at the top of the wall, who jumped with me below into the garden, and *the wolf* followed with much expedition. We then broke into a lonely avenue, which seemed to lead to some buildings or sheds at the back of the premises. The gipsies cast their eyes up first at the windows at the back of the house, and then listened outside the wall which divided the shed from the garden.

" ' All's safe !' remarked *the badger* in a whisper scarcely audible, ' the servants have all gone to rest long ago, and mother Zarah has well performed her business to day, or we should have heard old Rover before now !—now then for the window.'

" I now looked up, and for the first time beheld a casement in the wall, which was of extraordinary small dimensions, and was probably only meant to shed a light into a small enclosed yard. *The wolf* pulled forth his jemmy, and mounting on the shoulders of his companion, wrenched it open with very little difficulty, and without any noise.

" ' Now for the boy ;' said *the wolf*, in a whisper, and *the badger*, laying hold of my arm, with a very tight grasp, was preparing to lift me up to his companion, when with that tone of desperation which great anguish often imparts to the most imbecile person, I begged of him to have mercy on me, and not to suffer me to enter the house.

" ' Lift the devil's brat up,' said *the wolf* in a hoarse tone, ' and pay no attention to his tears. If he blubbers another word, damme but I will myself descend, and settle his business in no time.'

" The next moment I was lifted up to *the wolf*, who thrust me with some difficulty through the window, although at that time my form was very thin and diminutive.

" ' Have yer found th' ledge on th' other side ?' inquired *the wolf*, thrusting in his head.

" ' Yes,' I faintly articulated.

" ' Stop vhere yer are then for a minnit,' returned the robber, *badger*, have yer got th' lantern ready ?'

" ' Here it is,'' replied *the badger*, handing up the lantern which he had been illuminating during the time that *the wolf* was doing the other part of the business. *The wolf* handed me the lantern, aud said :—

" ' Yer can easily descend, for you'll find a short ladder underneath yer, it vos standing there this arternoon, so Zarah said : take th' lantern, and opposite to yer yer'll see two or three steps, vhich descend into a small area, vhere there is a low wooden door vhich is never bolted, and opens vith a latch. Vhen yer have opened that door, yer'll find yerself in a small vash-house, cross that, and ascend a flight of stairs vhich yer'll find opposite to yer, after yer quit th' vash-house ; them here steps vill conduct yer along a passage to th' hall, and yer can easily stand on th' form in th' hall, and reach th' bolt of th' door, let us in, an' yer vork vill be done. Now do yer understand vot I have said to yer ?'

" I answered tremulously in the affirmative.

" ' Werry vell, then,' whispered the villain, ' mind how you act, or it will be a bad night's vork for yer, that's all. You'd better take off yer shoes afore yer ascends th' stairs, and then no von vill hear yer. Ve shall be vaiting round at th' front o' th' house for yer opening th' door, an' if it is not done in less than five minutes, vhy I shall just take th' liberty—but never mind, yer understand me ; now then, avay yer go, all right !'

" With these villanous directions, *the wolf* made a rough motion for me to obey his mandates, and finding me hesitate—for I was so bewildered, terrified, and confused, that I scarcely knew what I did—he once more significantly presented the pistol to my view, and scowled in a ferocious and threatening manner upon me. This was enough ; made passive by fear, I stepped on the ladder, which I found in the situation that had been described, and the next moment I alighted on the pavement beneath.

" ' It's all right,' I heard *the wolf* whisper to his companion ; ' th' boy is safe below !'

" I now paused to recover myself from the state of confusion I was in, and looked timidly around me, expecting—nay, almost wishing—every moment to see some person rush out and seize me; but even in that case my fate would doubtless have been certain, for it is not probable that the villains would have made their escape until they had effectually silenced a witness who could so easily have betrayed their iniquitous schemes, and have brought them to justice. I ventured to raise my eyes once more towards the casement, and beheld the savage countenance of *the wolf* still there, and levelling the pistol towards me.

"'D—n yer, yer obstinate young thief!' he exclaimed in a loud whisper, 'vy d'yer pause? Another second, and I'll blow yer brains out! Th' steps—the steps opposite—can't yer see 'em?'

"This recalled me to a sense of my danger, and, with a sinking heart, I made towards the steps which led into the area, ever and anon looking behind me to see if the robber was still watching me, and finding a confirmation of my worst surmises, I opened the door, passed through the wash-house, and arrived at the foot of the staircase which led into the hall. Here I recollected the instructions *the wolf* had given me, to take off my shoes, and did so accordingly. I then held the lantern over my head to see that all was secure above, and seeing nothing but the dim shadow of my own figure on the wainscot, I began to ascend the stairs with a noiseless tread. When I reached the hall, I once more paused and looked around me; there was a wide stone staircase behind me, which led up to the apartments of the building, and the passage before me was lighted by a lamp suspended from the roof. All was still as death; to me, at that moment, that silence seemed particularly awful. It was the prelude, perhaps, of an eternal silence to more than one unfortunate and innocent being, and I was the instrument employed to effect that dreadful purpose. Again I hesitated, and at first had almost come to the determination of ascending the stairs, alarming the inmates of the mansion, and revealing the whole of the hideous plot; but a strange and unaccountable feeling

tempted me to abandon this praiseworthy design, and I moved silently towards the hall-door. I heard voices without, and again paused, and hid my lantern in my bosom, sinking down on the form with terror. Suddenly, however, I concluded that in all probability it was the two ruffians, and, gaining more courage, I placed my lips to the keyhole, and said, in a faint voice:—

"'Who's there?'

"'Vy, 'tis us to be sure,' replied *the wolf*, 'd'yer mean to keep us here for ever? you shall pay for this; make haste and unbolt the door!'

"I trembled so violently, that it was with extreme difficulty I could draw back the bottom bolt, and I then got upon the form and endeavoured to withdraw the one at the top. This was much larger and harder to remove than the other, and I made the attempt for some time in vain.

"'D—n yer!' again uttered *the wolf*, 'what a noise you are making.'

"'I can't pull the bolt back,' I fearfully replied.

"'Put some elbow-grease to it, yer lazy young brat,' replied *the wolf*.

"'Don't alarm the boy,' interposed *the badger*, in a somewhat milder tone than his companion; 'pull yer hardest, Jack, and don't funk over it.'

"I made a desperate effort, with the whole of the strength I could accumulate, and the bolt flew back with a squeaking sound. I then descended from the form, pulled back the latch, the door opened, and the two ruffians quickly entered the hall, and closed the door without the slightest noise after them. They both hastily pulled the black masks over their eyes, and then proceeded to lower the lamp in the hall and to extinguish it. After this, *the wolf* snatched the lantern from my hand, and grasped one of his pistols with the other.

"'Stay here with the boy!' said *the wolf*, in a whisper, 'I can do th' b'sness best by myself, but have your bull dogs ready in case they are wanted, now then, here goes, luck or no luck. Ten guineas to a dead monkey.'

"And with this very humourous speech, the robber, who had previously taken off his heavy boots, traversed the hall, and was soon lost, up the winding staircase, from the view.

"What a horrible moment of suspense was this to me; I felt my very heart's blood running cold through my veins, and I breathed hard and short. *The badger* held me with an iron grasp to prevent my attempting to fly, and after the elapse of a few moments of death-like silence, in which his impatience seemed excited to an almost insupportable degree, he advanced, drawing me with him to the foot of the staircase, where he listened. All was still—the robber mounted two or three stairs, when he again paused to listen. Suddenly a confused noise of the trampling of feet, broken and scarcely audible exclamations, and other sounds significant of a struggle, could be distinctly heard, *the badger* pressed my arm violently to enforce silence, and descending the stairs, pulled forth a long knife, forced me underneath his great coat, and crouched down behind the bannisters. The noise increased in loudness, and seemed to be approaching nearer, and at last we could plainly hear *the wolf's* horrid curses, which seemed to be excited by the resistance of some person to his nefarious attempts.—Another moment, and *the badger* was in the act of ascending the stairs, when the contending parties appeared at the top, and struggled violently to the bottom. *The wolf's* lantern fell to the floor, and its unextinguished rays, revealed to me the form of an aged-gray-headed but powerful man, in *deshabille*, who was struggling desperately with the robber.

"'*Badger*' exclaimed the wretch in a tone of phrenzy, 'come to my aid, or by hell th' old 'un will prove vun too many for me!—D——yer take yer hand from my throat!'

"At that awful moment *the badger* presented himself, leaving me bent double and nearly fainting behind the bannisters!—I saw him raise his arm, and aim a violent blow with the knife at the old man. I hid my eyes with a sickly, choking, sensation;—a cry of agony followed the action, and the voice of *the wolf* ejaculated;

"'Damnation! yer have plunged yer knife into my shoulder instead o' th' old scoundrel!—Quick! quick! to his heart! or by h—— we are lost!'

"Another horrible moment, and one deep, one agonized groan smote my ears then followed the heavy fall of some weighty body; I cast my eyes fearfully down, and beheld the poor old gentleman a bloody corpse at the foot of the staircase.

"'He's done for,' exclaimed *the wolf*, 'and d—n me if yer hav'n't almost settled my b's'ness too—quick, yer shawl!'

"The badger hastily handed his companion the shawl from off his neck, who twisted it around his shoulder as well as he could.

"'Now then, we must be off,' said *the wolf*, 'or it vill be *cold meat* for us.'

"'Where's the *swag*?' inquired the murderer, in a hoarse and dreadful whisper.

"'I've got it all right,' replied *the wolf*.

"He was interrupted by a strange noise which seemed to proceed from the gallery above, and then the sound of many feet were heard.

"'They've got th' scent,' exclaimed *the wolf*.

"'Quick, then! we have no time to lose!' answered *the badger*.

"'Where's the kid?' cried *the wolf*.

"'He's here,' replied the assassin, dragging me forth. Oh, how I recoiled from his touch. The noise now appeared nearer, and just as we gained the step of the hall-door outside, lights and a number of persons were visable on the top of the stairs. The ruffians hastily pulled me after them, and the door slammed-to with a loud noise. *The badger* caught me up in his arms, and they both fled across the wooden bridge, through the dark road, across the village, and getting into the fields, they threw themselves among some thick furze, which concealed us from all observation, and, with panting hearts, endeavoured to rest themselves after the great and awful exertions they had undergone.

"'It is a d——d dear-earned job,' whispered *the wolf*, with a half-supressed groan, from the pain he felt in the wound *the badger* had accidentally given him; 'who'd a thought th' old feller vould ha' been so tough?'

" 'There will be a fine row about this concern in no time,' cried *the badger;* ' the whole country will be up in arms, and if we don't cut our luckies pretty quick, th' traps vill nail us as sure as nuts. Our comrades will have struck all the tents, and have prepared every thing for our flight, before we get back, so we had better not lie sneaking here, unless we would have a lodging for nothing betwixt stone walls.'

" 'Jack,' said *the wolf* to me, perceiving that I was trembling with horror, ' you are now made one o' us, and cannot—or dare not—*peach;* if you vos to attempt it, you vould get scragged yerself, so let's ha' no more o' yer funking,

or ve must try vot a little beating vill do for yer.'

" 'Oh, pray let me go,' I exclaimed piteously; ' pity a poor friendless boy, whose feelings revolt from such dreadful proceedings he has this night witnessed; let me go about my business, and although I know it will be sinful to do so, yet I am willing to take any oath, never to reveal, by a single word or action, the dreadful events I have this night beheld.'

" 'Ha! ha! ha!' laughed the ruffian wolf; ' a fine yarn truly, but it's no go, my young 'un. Your fate is now linked vith ours, and it is o' no use yer trying to escape from it; but vot need you be in sich a funk about? yer didn't murder the old fool, and it vill be nothin' at all vhen yer used to it. But hark! is not them 'ere voices? Ve must be off, or ve shan't have a chance o' makin' our escape shortly.—Come along, *badger*.'

"With these words both the villains arose from the furze, and dragging me after them, we proceeded on a sharp run, till I was quite exhausted and ready to sink to the earth. At length we reached the entrance of the forest, and there we met the whole of the gang, with the tents and every thing packed up ready for travelling. The fatal consequences that had resulted from the burglary seemed to alarm them, but the booty which *the wolf* had concealed in the pockets of his great coat, soon appeased their fears, and having applied some herbs to the wound of *the wolf*, and given him and *the badger* a slight change of apparel, they proceeded to separate themselves different roads, having fixed upon a part of the country where they should meet together on the following night, and arrange for their future encampment. *The badger* and *the wolf*, taking me under their protection, agreed to travel together, and we started on our journey, although I declared that I felt so tired that I could not proceed much further. We travelled all the most unfrequented and dreary roads, avoiding the towns and villages, and at length day began faintly to dawn upon the eastern hills, and the ruffians began to consult together as to their future plans, they thinking it would not be safe to travel in the open day.

"'If ve could only reach Tim Jackson's,' observed *the wolf*, 'we might there rest ourselves for a few hours in safety.'

"'That's true,' replied *the badger*; 'but then it is fifteen miles to Tim's yet, and I am devilish tired. As for the boy, he is quite knocked up, and moves his legs as if there were chain cables affixed to each of them.'

"'If ve get into the high road,' said *the wolf*, 'and that vill be safe enough, I think, in this 'ere quarter, ve may p'r'aps get a lift in some cart or vaggin.'

"'So ve may,' observed *the badger*, 'let's get into the road.'

"We took a short cut across the fields we were in, the gipsies sprang over a hedge, lifting me after them, and we found ourselves in the high road, and shortly afterwards perceived an empty cart coming at no great distance behind us, with a sturdy-looking countryman plodding heavily by the side of the horse's head, smacking his whip and singing and whistling a simple country song by turns. My companions waited for the cart coming up, and then *the badger* addressed the driver in a disguised voice :—

"'Good morning, mate!'

"The driver reiterated the compliment, and after having hastily but not inquisitively surveyed our persons, resumed his whistling, and was proceeding on his way without taking any further notice of us.

"'It's a cold morning, countryman,' said *the badger*.

"'Hoy,' replied the driver, in a slow lazy tone of voice, 'but it be main foin weather for th' toime o' yeer, lad.'

"'Going to M———?' inquired the gipsy.

"'Hoy, I be gwain' to th' Wullpack Inn at there,' answered the countryman.

"'I'll stand some yale, lad,' said *the badger*, in a broad north-country dialect, 'if thee'lt gi'e us a lift on th' road.'

"'Hoy, to be zure wull I," answered the driver, apparently exhilirated at the prospect of the ale which *the badger* had promised him; 'jump up, my lads— thee't oot yarly this maunin'.'

"'Yees,' replied *the badger*, 'we ha' been travellin' th' whole o' th' neet, an' we be main fagged loike; but we must reach M——— yarly, acause we be gwain' to wurk loike.'

"'Hoy, hoy,' replied the waggoner, as *the badger* and *the wolf* jumped up into the cart.

"'Shall I reach th' lad up in th' cart to ye?' asked the driver; 'th' poor bairn do zeem nation tired.'

"'Yees, my son be a weakly bairn loike,' answered *the badger*, with well-acted dissimulation; 'an' oi an' his uncle here be not in a much better state: but needs must, thee knows, when the devil drives.'

" ' Reet, reet, measter,' remarked the countryman, handing me into the cart; *the badger* placed me between himself and *the wolf*, on some sacks, among which they had ensconced themselves, whispered to me to be cautious, the waggoner smacked his whip, the cart moved on, and the driver, resuming his whistling, took no further notice of us. *The badger* very quickly composed himself to sleep, *the wolf* was in a half restless sort of doze, and, tired completely with the unexampled exertions, both of body and mind, I had undergone for the last six or seven hours, I gradually sunk into a deep sleep. But troubled and wretched was that sleep; my disturbed imagination recalled to my mind in my visionary state, all the horrible transactions of the night; once more I beheld the villain plunge his knife into the poor old man's side; again I heard his expiring groans, and saw his bleeding and mangled form stretched upon the earth. Then the scene changed, and I beheld myself in a dungeon, loaded with fetters; a person in black entered—he read to me an order for my execution, for participating in the assassination of the old gentleman. Once more the scene changed, and I found myself forced along by the officers of justice, through several dark and lengthy stone passages, until we arrived in the open air, and there three gallowses met my appalled gaze, from two of which were already suspended the writhing forms of *the wolf* and *the badger*. I imagined that I was led beneath the unoccupied gallows, placed in a cart, and put into the hands of the terrible-looking executioner. I heard the clergyman read the last solemn service, I felt the halter placed around my neck, the cap drawn over my eyes, and——but I cannot proceed with all the horrors that tormented my sleeping faculties on that occasion, nor should I have been so particular in describing them so far, knowing that they cannot prove very interesting to you, only that I am anxious to convince the public—who, from the curious papers of this immortal society, will at some future period become acquainted with my adventures—that it was no ordinary event, no common every-day occurrence,

that ultimately made me become a member of that vagrant body I feel proud to acknowledge."

Here Jack once more paused in his truly interesting and most remarkable history, and received the plaudits of his delighted listeners; after which he moistened his throat with a copious draught of punch, and resumed his tale :—

" How long I had slept I can't say, but I was aroused by some one pulling me roughly by the arm, and, with a cry of terror, I started up and looked around me, expecting a realisation of part, if not the whole of my dream. I found that the cart had stopped before the door of an inn, that *the wolf* had already alighted, and was talking to the driver, and *the badger* was preparing to do the same. He muttered an oath at the expression of my terror, and cast a look upon me which quickly recalled me to a full recollection of the peculiarity of my situation.

" ' Whoy, *Dick*, lad !' said he, addressing himself to me in his assumed tone of voice, ' thee'st slept all thee brains away, arn't thee, lad ?—Come, get thee oot o' th' cart.'

" I complied with this order, and *the badger* quickly followed me, and advanced to the countryman and *the wolf*.

" ' Well, Ralph,' said *the badger* to *the wolf*, ' hast thee gi'en th' money for th' yale to un ?'

" ' Yees, Roger,' replied *the wolf*, also assuming with much skill the Yorkshire dialect.

" ' That be reet, mun,' exclaimed *the badger*, ' come along, then, we mun be ganging noo.—Good boi, lad !'

" ' Thee'dst better ha' some o' the yale,' observed the driver.

" ' Nou, nou, thankee, lad,' replied *the badger*, ' we mun stop noo !' And at the end of this colloquy the countryman entered the inn to get his ale, and we proceeded on our journey.

" We walked for about half an hour over fields and through bye lanes, and at last we reached a very mean and retired village, with only a few low wooden huts, which I afterwards found were inhabited chiefly by smugglers, with which that part of the country, in those days, was very much infested. At the top of this secluded village we stopped before the door of a cottage, the smoke from the chimney of which gave notice that the inmates were up, notwithstanding it was still very early.

" 'It's all right, there's some vun here,' remarked *the wolf*, and with that he gave three heavy knocks on the door with the head of a large thick stick which he carried along with him. No answer was returned until the gipsy had repeated the knocks, when a casement above was thrown open, and a man about fifty, with a hardy, deep-lined, weather-beaten countenance—which was amply supplied with a pair of huge red whiskers, that met together under his chin—thrust forth his head and demanded to know who was there, and what they wanted.

" 'All right, Tim; it's only I and *the badger*,' answered *the wolf*, raising his head and revealing his countenance to the inquirer.

" 'Hollo! what the devil brings you here at this time of the morning?' exclaimed the man, taking in his head before he could receive an answer to his inquiry.

" 'Jack, open the door, yer lubberly swab,' we then heard him say to some person inside, and a heavy foot approached the door and opened it, giving us admittance. The person who had opened the door was a youth with a dark, surly, and unprepossessing countenance, curiously dressed, half sailor, half landsman fashion, who seemed as though he had been but recently aroused from a comfortable nap. We were shown into a dirty, smoky room, with only a couple of chairs, several kegs lying about, and the fire-place decorated with numerous pipes, tobacco-boxes, pouches, and cocoa-nuts, and before we could take a seat, the individual who had addressed us from the window, entered the room, smoking a Dutch pipe.

" He was a tall, stout, robust man, attired in a Guernsey striped shirt, a large jacket over it, a pair of huge boots upon his legs, a broad leathern belt, with a large buckle in front round his waist, and a striped woollen cap upon his head. He advanced towards *the wolf* and the other gipsy, with a rough but cordial expression of welcome, and then commanded the youth in a surly tone to bring out the bottle, pipes, and " weed," who having departed to fulfil his desires, Tim inquired the cause of their unexpected visit. The gipsies satisfied him upon such points as they deemed necessary, wisely concealing the more serious portion of the business, and in order to conciliate Tim's good will, presented him with a handsome gold watch, being part of the booty of the previous night's burglary. This timely present seemed to have the desired effect, and Tim expressed his wishes to serve them in any way that came within his power. The ruffians replied that they only wanted a few hours rest, and at night a boat, and the services of Tim to row them over to B—, whence they could proceed to meet their comrades according to appointment. This point being settled, Tim inquired whether they would not take something to eat, and on the gipsies replying in the affirmative, the before mentioned youth was once more despatched to the room up stairs to procure the provisions, and soon returned bringing with him a very tempting looking piece of *corn beef* with vegetables, and also some dried fish. Previous to their repast, however, the gipsies were anxious to try the quality of the liquor Tim had in the bottle, a request which was immediately complied with, and both *the wolf* and *the badger* drank no less than three glasses each of the hollands, before they commenced eating.

" 'Come, my lad,' said Tim to me, ' you must be hungry with your journey, so fall to, and eat as long as you like.'

" 'However, I was too much troubled, and too ill with what I had undergone to feel the cravings of hunger, although it was so many hours since I had tasted any kind of refresment, and I meekly begged to be excused from joining in the repast.

" 'Eat you obstinate young fool!' said *the wolf* in his usual savage manner; ' I tell yer vot it is, master Jack, I shall have no more o' your nonsense, and if yer attempts it, I shall be under th' *painful* necessity o' breakin' o' yer neck! yer'd better eat!'

"This *affectionate* promise frightend me, and I complied as well as I was able, although it was very little I could eat, and every mouthful seemed like poison to me. The gipsies having made a hearty meal, filled the Dutch pipes which Tim had given them, and set down to smoke and drink, seeming to have forgotten the purpose for which they had partly come there, namely, to get a few hours repose previous to their resuming their journey.

"'The boy seems ill and tired,' said the smuggler, who beneath a rough covering seemed to possess a more humane heart than belongs to many persons holding a more virtuous situation; —' he is very young and weak, and too much may knock him up, so suppose you send him to bed until you are ready to depart.' The gipsies, who were nearly intoxicated, did not object to this proposal.

"'He had better take Jack's hammock up stairs!' observed Tim; 'Jack, shew the youngster up stairs, and see him all safe.' The gipsies, had they been sober, would probably not have been so impolitic as to suffer me out of their sight, but they were too much engaged in drinking and smoking to think any thing at all about the matter, and I was committed to the care of my namesake, who bid me follow him.

"I confess, at that very moment a hope, wild as it may appear to be, sprung up in my bosom, that this chance might afford me the means of escape, and I resolved to run every risk to effect it, if there was any possibility of my getting away from a situation so dreadful as the one I was then placed in. After ascending a dark and short flight of stairs, or rather a ladder, we entered through a trap-door in the floor, a small and dreary looking room, in which a couple of seamen's hammocks were slung, and no doubt were the beds of Tim and his son. There was a back window to the room as well as a front one, and this circumstance also increased my hopes, and I awaited impatiently the departure of the smuggler's son, to see whether my projects would be likely to be available.

"I will not take the trouble to undress myself;" said I, "then I shall be ready when it is time for us to quit the hut."

"'Very well,' replied the youth, assisting me into the hammock, and afterwards leaving the room, shutting the door after him, and retiring with a heavy tread down the stairs to rejoin his father and the two *worthy* persons who called him friend. No sooner had he gone than I got hastily out of the hammock, and first taking the precaution to listen at the room door, to find if all was safe, I approached the back window, and examined the prospect beyond!—My heart palpitated so with mingled hope and fear, that it was with the utmost difficulty I could support myself. At length, I regained my firmness, and once more cast my eyes from the casement, which I hoped would afford me the means of making my escape. I discovered that it looked upon the sea beach, and in the distance the broad expanse of the ocean, calm as an infant's slumber, met my anxious eyes glittering in the rays of the morning sun. There was no person moving on the beach, but at the distance many a smack and gallant vessel at anchor met my gaze.

"I now beheld that all the sanguine expectations I had entertained were likely to be accomplished, and with the most inexpressible delight, I contemplated the delightful prospect before me, the prospect to liberty. From the casement to the beach beneath, it was no great distance, but still it was too much to leap, and I returned into the room to see whether I could find any thing to accelerate my descent. I listened attentively at the door for a few minutes to hear whether the fellows were all safe below, and could hear their loud laughter, which assured me that they were too much occupied with their own conversation and the exhilerating efforts of the Hollands to give a singal thought to any thing else, and I determined to lose no time while such a favourable opportunity for me to escape presented itself. I therefore returned back from the door, and was looking for something to aid me in my descent from the window, when I beheld upon the floor, just beneath the hammock in which I imagined that the elder smuggler slept, a canvass bag, such as seamen often carry their money in. My curiosity was, of course, excited to see what the bag contained, and I determined to satisfy it. First, however, I had the precaution to pile every article of furniture I could find against the room door to prevent any hasty intrusion of the wretches below, ere I could put my designs into execution, and then with a trembling hand, I untied the piece of tape with which the bag was bound round, and to my amazement beheld several pieces of silver, which at that time I knew not the names of, but the value of which I was thoroughly aware of; I had never beheld so much wealth before in my life. With delighted eyes I looked upon this glittering treasure, which I readily imagined belong to the smuggler, and had been accidentally dropt by him in getting in or out of the hammock. Of what infinite assistance a treasure like this would be to me in my flight, I reflected,—and as I reflected, I turned the money out of the bag and counted it over several times, every time it appeared more dazzling to my eyes; but then I thought to myself, would it not be dishonest in me to appropriate that to my own use, which was the property of another!—I paused, and with a sigh of regret, threw the bag with its contents upon the spot where I had found it, and was proceeding with a rope I had just found, to make good my descent from the window, when again the temptation to take the money occurred to me;—I reflected upon the dangerous journey I was about to undertake, and the vicissitudes, privations, and miseries I should be exposed to without money or friends; besides, how did I know that the money actually belonged to Jackson, or, if indeed it was his now by the right of possession, it was more than probable he had obtained it in a dishonest manner, and therefore he had no more claim upon it than myself. It is astonishing how soon a mind upon the verge of ruin, or naturally prone to vice can find sophistry to uphold its logic, and I afforded a very fair example of this truth; I put the money in my pocket, and thus committed the first dishonest action of my life. But this was no time for further reflection, another minute, and my designs to escape might be rendered abhortive, and myself dreadfully punished for having dared to make the attempt, I therefore immediately proceeded to render my flight secure.

" I fastened one end of the rope to a staple which I found in the window-post, and then fastening the other round my body, I boldly flung myself from the casement, and alighted in safety below. Here I awaited not a minute, you may be sure, but releasing my body from the rope, I took that road which I remembered I had come in company with *the badger* and *the wolf*, and with breathless haste I ran along, and was soon out of sight of the smuggler's hovel."

Scapegrace Jack having arrived at this part of his curious recital, we must take the liberty of concluding the present chapter, which has already extended beyond our usual limits; the reader will therefore be pleased to look for the relation of those remarkable incidents, which we promised to narrate in this chapter, in our next.

CHAP. V.

JACK'S ADVENTURES ARE TERMINATED—EVERY PARTICULAR PROMISED IN OUR LAST CHAPTER DETAILED HERE—INTERESTING ACCOUNT OF JACK'S JOURNEY TO LONDON—A NIGHT'S LODGING IN A CADGERS' SNOOZING KEN, AND THE COMPANY WHICH JACK FALLS INTO, WHICH IS THE OCCASION OF HIS INTRODUCTION TO THE BEGGARS' HAUNT, AND THE FINAL POLISH TO HIS EDUCATION.

" IT was a beautiful day, although extremely cold, and the red gleam of the sum streamed in a flood of glory over the ice-bound earth, and glittered among the icicles which, in spite of the warmth of his rays, still clung to each leafless bough. Fearful that my flight might be discovered, I continued to run along as fast as my limbs could carry me, until, completely exhausted, I could proceed no farther; and, hastening into a field by the road-side, I seated myself behind a thickset hedge, and sought to recover myself. I knew it would not be safe to remain long where I was, for should the ruffians discover my flight, they would not fail immediately to pursue me, and probably sacrifice me to their rage, or their fears of my ultimately succeeding in my endeavours to escape, and revealing their crimes. I therefore once more counted over the money I had found, and having tied it up securely in the bag, I thrust it into my jacket pocket, and prepared to start once more upon my journey.

" With an idea of baffling the scent of the wretches, should they pursue me, I struck into a path across the fields, and soon found myself in a wild and unfrequented part of the country. I had not the slightest idea of the direction in which I was going, but was fortunate enough in having chosen the right way; for, after I had passed several hours in traversing extensive fields, dreary lanes, and crossing lofty hills, I had the pleasure once more to find myself in the high road, and in a few minutes afterwards I beheld the London mail rolling rapidly along the road. I was now extremely hungry, and perceiving a village at no great distance, I determined to venture into a house, and try to get some refreshment.

" Previous to arriving at the village, however, I had the presence of mind to take from the bag in my pocket, the smallest of the coins, fearful that if the guests at the house I might call, should see the whole of the contents of my bag, they might suspect my honesty, and it might lead to the most painful results. As it afterwards appeared to me, it was a very fortunate thing that this idea occurred to me, or I should probably have lost the whole, and perhaps have been sent to prison into the bargain.

" Having arrived at the village, I entered the only tavern it contained, and after asking the landlord, a surly looking man, who eyed me with a scrutinizing and suspicious look, for some refreshment, I made my way into a dirty and old fashioned looking parlour, in which there were a number of men assembled, most of them mechanics apparently, but two of these individuals engaged my attention particularly. They were two stout, and stern looking men, attired in large rough top coats and carried with them several bladders which appeared to be filled with something that pleased the palates of the guests, for they severally tipped the men a small sum of money, upon which a quill was applied to the neck of the bladder, and they were allowed to suck at it for a short time, a privilege which seemed to afforded them the most luxurious enjoyment. These men I afterwards learned were smugglers, and so much was that part of the country infested with them, that they came to the towns and villages, with impunity, and disposed of their contraband articles in the manner I have described. In fact, in those days, there was scarcely the keeper of a public house in that part of the country, who was not connected with smuggling.

" The company gazed upon me with curious eyes, when I entered the room, and I soon perceived that I was in bad quarters, and was anxious to get out of them as soon as possible. When the landlord brought me in what I had ordered he gazed at me with still more curiosity, and awaited for the money which I gave him, and he had the honesty to give me the change. He then left the room muttering something between his teeth which I could not hear, but it more than ever convinced me of the necessity of my leaving as soon as I could. I was not long in despatching my frugal meal, and then bowing timidly to the company, and thanking the landlord, who said nothing, but looked with increase suspicion towards me, I hastened from the house, and pursued my way with renewed vigour. It was now getting late; the sun had sunk behind the western hills, and twilight was fast succeeding; the wind began to blow very cold, and drifted the snow which was lying thick upon the earth, in mountainous heaps across my path. I paused, and began to think within myself, what I had best do. To proceed much farther, I felt myself totally unable, for I had already travelled a very great distance, and when it is recollected that I had had but very little rest since the fatigue of the previous night, it will not be wondered that I should now feel tired. Besides I was fearful to travel at night, lest I might fall into as bad company as that I had escaped from, and to attempt to sleep in the open air would have been worse than madness, as I must undoubtedly have been frozen to death; I therefore determined to make the best of my way to the nearest town, and making up some plausible tale, put up at some public house for the night, and resume my journey by the break of day in the morning. Just after I had come to this resolution, the tinkling bells of some waggoner's horses vibrated in my ears, and shortly afterwards I could hear the heavy wheels rolling over the hard, frozen earth. I stopped, resolved to inquire of the waggoner how far it was to the next town. I had not to wait long, the waggon approached, and I went up to the man and put the question I had designed to him. The man, who had a good humoured, healthy countenance, looked at me a minute or two intently, and then said:—

"'Whoy lad thee'st canna trudge all't way to next toon t' night!—whoy it be ten mile I reckon, and thee seem'st tired already; but if thee loikes thee canst tumble into the waggon, an' I will tak' thee there an' welcome.'

"In tones of the utmost sincerity I expressed my gratitude to the good natured countryman, and was then assisted by him into the waggon, in which I found a man and his wife and two children, who looked very poor people, and were all fast asleep. Feeling myself secure, I rolled myself amongst some loose hay, and quickly dropped off to sleep, from which I did not awaken until I was aroused by the waggoner, the waggon having arrived at the town, and the place of its destination. I entered the inn where the waggon stopped, and representing myself as a poor boy, who was travelling to join my parents at a distant part of the country, I found no difficulty in procuring a lodging for the night, and after warming myself by the cheerful blaze of the parlor fire, I was

shewn up to the room in which I was to repose. It had two very clean beds in it, but neither of them were occupied, and feeling myself secure, I returned my thanks to Providence for my fortunate escape from the gipsies, and then with a more contented mind than I had for a long time before enjoyed, I retired to repose, and slept soundly till the morning's sun darted its rays in at the casements of my chamber. I arose very much refreshed, and going down stairs, I found the inmates of the inn already stirring, and having partaken of a hearty breakfast, I started on my journey.

"I should become tedious, were I to trouble you with all the particulars of my toilsome pilgrimage; suffice it to say that after a week's travelling, I found myself in Whitechapel about the middle of a very dreary and rainy day. My emotions upon first beholding the great metropolis, were of the most extraordinary nature. I looked around me, and I thought the scene the most wonderful I had ever beheld, the numerous and lengthy streets; the crowds of people bustling to and fro, all evidently intent upon business; the noisy rattling of the different vehicles, the variety and magnificence of the shops, and the curious cries of the various itinerant merchants, excited my utmost astonishment and delight. "Surely," I thought to myself, "in such a place as this it is impossible for a person to remain long without finding employment." And I congratulated myself on the determination I had made to make it the place of my destination.

"I was in London, it is true, but now I had arrived there, I was puzzled as to what should be my future designs; where was I to go?—What was I to do? How get employment, and what kind of employment did I consider myself fit for; I confess I knew not how to answer those questions, but it was not long before I laughed at my ignorance; it was a very short time before I was completely initiated into the grand art and mystery of living in London without working; and I must say taking the obscurity and the difference of my former life into consideration, I received my accomplishments with great readiness.

"I had husbanded my money remarkably well, and had yet nine or ten of the largest pieces of coin, which I now knew to be half crowns, in the canvass bag, which I thought would be quite sufficient to keep me until I could procure some kind of employment. Without coming to any decision, I wandered about the streets the whole of the day, constant novelty of every thing I beheld withdrawing my thoughts from the real misery of my situation; and towards night I found myself in Field Land, and feeling tired, began to think of procuring a lodging for the night. I made inquiries of a dirty and ugly looking old Jewess, who was the proprietor of a shop in which were exhibited a profusion of silk handkerchiefs of various colours, sizes, and patterns, and she directed me to a house a few doors past her own residence, in which she observed 'I should be plantifully *hacomidated and sheap !*'—Thanking her for her information, I hastened towards the house she had pointed out, which was one of those ruinous old lath and plaster reliques of former days, remarkable for their filth, with which that curious neighbourhood abounds, laconically announcing on a dirty canvas in the window, "*Lodgings!*" I had no occasion to knock at the door

No. 8.

for that was very accomodating by standing open, and I entered a passage which as well as the scanty light which was admitted to it would allow, exhibited the dirty marks of many muddy feet, and stunk most dreadfully. I was not much gratified with the appearance of the place, and was half inclined to hasten from it without making any application, when a loud laugh reverberated in my ears, and a door at the side of the passage opening, a short dirty, looking, woman, issued forth with a lamp in one hand and an empty quart pot in the other.

" 'Hollo! who the devil are you?' said the woman, observing me in the passage, and thrusting the lamp in my face to take a more minute scrutiny of my features. I stated my business briefly, and taking one more hasty but critical view of my person, which seemed not to displease her, she desired me in rather civiler accents to walk into the parlour. I obeyed. The place which had been designated a parlour by the woman, exhibited nothing more prepossessing than the exterior of the house; it was a miserable, dirty, large, and clumsy looking room, exhibiting the laths in various parts of the walls, while the other portions of it would convince even an indifferant observer, that spiders were allowed to colonize themselves there in undisturbed security, The ceiling was black with smoke, and the floor was covered with coarse sand, which was made to supply the place of a carpet, or the superfluous trouble of scouring it. The furniture consisted of one arm chair, three smaller ones, a table of painted deal, and a chest of drawers, all in a state of the utmost imbecillity. Upon my entrance into the room, I had been quite unable to distinguish any objects for smoke, and upon that dispersing, I discovered that it proceeded from the lips of two grimey faced, black chinned, gentlemen, who monopolized both corners of a good fire, and were evidently quite at home, but anxiously awaiting the woman's return with the replenished quart pot. They half rose from their seats, and winked at each other when they recognized me, and seemed half inclined to give utterance to some

choice witticism with which their brains were amply stored, when they were stopped by a significant glance from the landlady, as I soon found out the before mentioned woman was, who with some degree of politeness desired me to sit down by the fire till she returned with the beer for her friends. Not much liking the appearance of the two men, I took a seat at some distance from the fire, and they having amply indulged themselves in surveying my person, applied themselves more vigorously to their pipes.

" 'A good trump mother Botts!' observed one of the men, breaking the silence they had before maintained, 'never no occashun to vant a drain if yer can only get on th' right side on her.'

" 'You're right, Joe,' replied the other, 'mother Botts is nothin' else but *jonuck,* and yet I vonder at it for she does get chizzled nicely at times; vy I owes her no less than a *couter* now for the *doss.*'

" 'An' werry proper too;' remarked the first speaker, 'there's nuffin like runnin' a score vith people; it makes 'em respect yer so much; vy, if it varnt for owing 'em ochre, many on 'em vouldn't be werry glad to see us; yer see it's hope that keep 'em civil; they hopes by that here ve shall pay 'em some time or other, an' so they are werry glad to see us.'

" 'Vot a precious vile Mother Bott's is gone;' said the second speaker, without making any remark upon the sage observations of his friend; but his impatience was quickly gratified by the lady whose merits they had been so ably discussing, with a pot of beer, which she placed upon the table before them, and then turned to me and said :—

" 'So, my dear, you want a bed, do you?'

" I replied in the affirmative.

" 'Vell and vot figger vill yer go to, my dear?' again said the worthy hostess, looking inquisitively at my dust colored clothes and my sun burnt features.

" I expressed my ignorance of her meaning, upon which the two gentlemen in the corner, indulged in a short laugh, and mutual expressions of "*green!*" "*yokel!*" "*joskin!*" and other expressive terms, all at that time equally inexplicable to me. Mrs. Botts, however, quickly silenced them by artful winks, and plainly inquired what price I could afford go to. I informed her of my ignorance of the charge for a lodging.

"'Ah! poor child,' said she, with much apparent kindness, 'I see you are not much awake to London, just come from the country, eh?' I nodded assent. 'Ah, poor thing,' resumed Mrs. Botts, 'I thought so; vell, it is a good job yer have come to me, for London is a very wicked place, and young gentlemen like you are often led astray and plundered by vicked people; but there is nothing o' that sort carried on in my hestablishment, for although I say it vot shouldn't say it, there is not a more respectable lodgin' house in all Chick Lane than mine, is there gentlemen?' The two gentlemen to whom this appeal was made, both expressed their concurrance, and exchanged a pleasant little smile between them.

"'Well, my dear,' continued the woman, 'as I suppose you a poor boy, I shall let you sleep in my best room and only charge you sixpence, which is only half what I charge regularly; but I always makes allowance for poor people, especially a poor young boy like you; you'll find it a werry select room I can sure yer, and there is only ten young gentlemen there yet, so you will be as snug and as comfortable as if you vos in a palace.'

"I expressed my thanks for this very remarkable kindness, and as I was anxious to get away from the presence of the two *gentlemen* in the corner, I requested that I might be shewn to the *select* apartment directly, as I was very tired.

"'Very well, my dear,' answered Mrs. Botts, and then added with a short cough, 'perhaps, young gentleman, you vill have no objection to pay me the sixpence now; not that I doubt your honesty, but yer see I makes it a reg'lar rule, and you know it von't do to break through the reg'lar rules!'

"Of course I could not object to these reasonable observations, and I began to feel for the money. My bag which contained the best part of my wealth, I had the precaution to conceal in my stocking, only extracting a half crown, which wa the smallest change I had, to provide for my present necessities, and which I gave to Mrs. Botts, requesting that she would give me the change. Mrs. Botts took the half crown with an avidity, which I acknowledge at the time seemed to me, rather extraordinary, jinked it on the table, and then bit it between her teeth, after which she calmly consigned it to her own pocket, and rummaged about in the same place for two or three seconds, but without seeming to gain any thing satisfactory to her researches.

"'Dear me,' said she, at last, in a tone of regret, 'I declare I thought I had got some small change, but I find I have nothing less than a guinea; what shall I do? Mr. Duckett, or Mr. Nobley you hasn't got change for a half crown, have yer?'

"The two interesting individuals to whom this question was addressed both declared upon their 'onner' they had nothing less than a *five pound note*.

"'Well, it ca'n't be helped,' said Mrs. Botts, 'I dare say th' young gentleman is not afraid to trust to my honesty till the mornin', it's werry awkward to be vithout change, but before you go avay in th' mornin', young man, be sure you don't forget to ax for yer two shillin's, it will be as safe as th' Bank of Hingland, von't it, gentlemen?'

"Messrs Nobley and Duckett both confirmed the assertions of Mrs. Botts by a vehement '*in course*,' and, of course, upon such unquestionable security, I had no reasonable cause to feel the slightest doubt, I therefore nodded my satisfaction, and followed the worthy landlady out of the room, a half suppressed chuckle between Messrs. Nobley and Duckett, meeting my ears as I quitted the apartment.

"I followed Mrs. Botts up a very wide and old-fashioned staircase, remarkably dirty and broken, until we reached a small landing, where four doors attracted my attention, from each of which loud peals of coarse laughter intermixed with certain peculiar expressions, which to my ears sounded like any thing but such as should be the spontaneous aspirations of young gentlemen, burst upon my ears.

" 'Dear me,' said Mrs. Botts, who doubtless remarked something very nearly appertaining to dissatisfaction depicted on my countenance, 'what a noise the young dogs are making; yer see they are all such very nice and merry young men, and they are so happy.'

"While Mrs. Botts had been making these observations, she had been in the act of extracting a large bunch of rusty keys from her pockets, one of which she applied to the padlock of the middle door, and which I must say gave me far from any favourable idea of the respectability or comfort of the lodgings she had been so profuse in her praise of.

" 'Yer see, my dear,' remarked Mrs. Botts, ' I am so careful of my lodgers that I always lock them in at night, and then there is no fear of any harm coming to them !'

"Before I could offer any reply to these observations, had I been prepared to do so, the door of the room was thrown open, I walked in, and before I had time to look about me, Mrs. Botts wished me a good night, retired, and the door was locked upon me.

" For a few minutes the sense of hearing was all I could indulge in, for the room was in a complete fog of tobacco smoke; but the sounds were of the most curious and conglomorated description, swearing, laughing, shouting, singing, and the rattling of many heavy shod feet, performing a pleasant and original series of Terpsichorean feats. At length the smoke partially evaporated, and the *coup d'œil* which burst upon my view, certainly surpassed every thing that I had ever before beheld. It would be perhaps unnecessary to enter into a particular description of the place I found myself in, to many of the learned *cadgers* present, who have often had the felicity of witnessing it themselves, but as there are a number of new members present who may know very little about these matters, I think it may be as well to give an exact picture of *a Cadger's Snoozing Ken* !

" I found myself in a room of considerable dimensions, and filled with smoke, cobwebs, and filth. It was dimly lighted by two half burnt out lamps, which cast a lurid glare upon the strange and almost inconceivable misery and strangeness of the place.

"Along each side of this curious apartment were spread upon the floor several coarse mattresses, redolent of filth and misery. In some instances they were occupied by two or three coarsely carved visaged individuals, some of whom gave notice from their nasal organs that in spite of the hubbub and riot which prevailed in the room, they were able to court Morpheus, while others were awake, and sitting up on the mattresses smoking short pipes, and displaying their colloquial powers with some ragged friend who held the tempting stimulant of a measure of gin in his hand. At one table was seated a party of boys, who were amusing themselves by a most spirited and well contested game at shove half-penny, while squatted on the floor, exactly opposite to them were two youths attired in short jackets not remarkable either for the quality of the materials of which they were made, or the fashion in which they were conceived. They were both greedily devouring a penny loaf each, and what they technically called a *'Dolphin,'* i. e. a red herring, and although they were not taking quite so active a part in the proceedings of the persons in the room, as to attract particular attention, they seemed to have the good opinion of the ragged faternity. At another part of the *chamber* (?) three or four fellows were displaying their abilities on *the light fantastic toe*, to the evident gratification of many individuals present, but to the very great annoyance of some persons who were domiciled in the adjoining apartment, and who might be heard knocking loudly against the wall, and requesting them in language not at all remarkable for its elegance, to make less noise, as it quite disturbed the ' *soft repose,*' of the respectable part of the community. To these expostulations, no attention was paid, and it seemed as if they had determined to annoy them the more, for speaking about it at all.

" Judge of my feelings upon being ushered into this loathsome and remarkable den; for a few minutes I was rivetted to the spot with confusion, from which having aroused myself, my fears held a predominant power over my mind, and I placed my hand upon the latch of the door, with an anxious wish to be enabled to make my escape, but in that hope I was disappointed—the door was secured outside, and I thus found myself a prisoner among a set of wretches who appeared to me no better than the gipsies from whom I had so providentially escaped. As soon as my presence was discovered in the room, there was a loud shout of "*a new chum*," and I was immediately subjected to an impudent scrutiny from each of the fellows, and also to many remarks which to me were quite unintelligible, but seemed to afford those who uttered them the most unbounded delight; it seemed to be a general opinion, however, that I was about as green as grass, and as flat as a pancake, which of course, with people of our highly respectable calling, are considered as indisputable licenses to victimizing on an unlimited scale. I therefore gave myself up for a fleeced one, and did not expect to leave the place with a single coin in my possession. I determined, however, to keep as close to my money as I could do with safety to myself, and congratulated myself highly on the foresight which had prompted me to conceal my treasure in my stocking. To go to rest, or rather to make an attempt to rest, I was resolved not to do; and I also resolved to try and muster up all the courage I possessed (which I must confess at that period was but a very small portion), and endeavour to show them by my conduct that I was not quite so *green* as they took me for. It will also be conceived by you all, that I now really began not to feel quite so simple as when I quitted the wretched hovel where I was born; the germs of natural sagacity which were implanted in my mind, began to expand themselves—besides, I had had some experience during the very short time I had been among the gipsies, and withal possessing a reflective mind, I was in a very promising way, with a little tuition, to make a proficient in the *honourable* art I was fated in future to practice.

"It is a most remarkable thing how soon a person may be tempted to swerve entirely from their former practices, if they make but one slip; and no person has ever afforded a more extraordinary instance of that fact than myself: but I do not regret the actions of my past life, inasmuch as they have afforded me unbounded amusement, experience, and riches, and also when I feel disinclined to enter into the more active spirit of our community, the adventures I have met with will afford me ample means of mental enjoyment, by recalling the reminiscences of my youth to my memory. But I am growing tedious. Wishing to appear as much at my ease as possible, knowing that that was the surest way of being suffered to remain there without annoyance, I calmly squatted myself down upon the floor by the side of the two *gentlemen* in the jackets, and pretended to take an idifferent survey of the apartment and its inmates. The two young gentlemen eyed me for a second or two closely, and then exchanged two or three significant glances with one another, as they proceeded to finish their anatomization of the red herring; they next extracted two short and blackened pipes from their jacket pockets, and taking forth a discoloured and rather ancient-looking tin box at the same time, proceeded to fill them with tobacco. All this time they showed from their expressive glances, that they had a peculiar wish to enter into a conversation with me, but were at a loss how;—not that I mean to insinuate from this that their conversational powers were of any mean order.

"At last, however, the eldest of them broke the ice by hoping I was well; that I seemed tired, looked as though I had been travelling, and then expressed the most unqualified disapprobation of the persons in the room, especially as regarded the reception of myself, and concluded a rather smart and spirited harrangue, by declaring 'that they couldn't abear any thin' in th' shape o' takin' an adwantage on a yokel, acause ve vere all *raw* vonce; but I needn't fear, for if any on 'em offered to insult me, they should feel the greatest pleasure in dislocating their nose, bunging up their eyes, or in fact, in doubling them up altogether.'

"The more to embellish this speech,

the young gentleman neatly finished it by asking me, in the most affable and modest manner imaginable, if I had the price of a pot that I could lend him *till the mornin'*, as his *bank* was low, and he was very thirsty with devouring the '*Dolphin.*' This request, although so civilly made, I was afraid that I should be under the painful necessity to refuse, for I had nothing but the cash concealed in my stocking (as I thought) at that time, and of course I had no particular inclination to entrust either of those young gentlemen with the secret of my hidden treasure. But happening to feel in all my pockets, I discovered some pence in the lining of my jacket which had before escaped my observation, and thinking it best to endeavour to conciliate the friendship of the two before-mentioned individuals while I remained with them, I did not hesitate in presenting them with the whole of the contents of my pocket, which gained for me many very flattering eulogiums from the respectable youths, all of which tended towards one grand and important conclusion—namely, that I was a d—d good *feller*, a compliment which I of course duly appreciated, and politely acknowledged. The gentleman whom I had thus accommodated, then rung a bell which I had not observed before, and in a short time the mistress of this very respectable establishment appeared at the door, and in a surly tone demanded the reason of the summons; the youth, winking significantly at her, requested a pot of beer, and she vanished to comply with his order, ere I could make known to her my opinion of the accommodation she had praised so much, and request permission to leave the house. The beer was speedily brought, and Mrs. Botts departed with the same haste, so that I found it would be useless to attempt to leave the place, and that I must be compelled to content myself as well as I could, till the morning would bring me liberty. My feelings were none of the most pleasant nature, you may be certain; for the lodgers, having exhausted themseves by rioting, had some of them fallen off to sleep, while the rest sat down and began to relate to one another various curious anecdotes of their lives, deeds, and avocations, which gave me no very high opinion of their characters, and convinced me that they were none of them too honest, and got their livings in the best way they could, either by cadging, or begging, or *borrowing.*

" The two individuals who so particularly *honoured* me by their attention I elicited by their conversation were members of a beggars' club, and had figured with some *eclat* at many of the principal prisons in London. They tried by various artful means to elicit from me where I had come from, whether I had any money, and what were my intentions in London. In these efforts they were successsful enough to learn from me that I had come to London for the purpose of obtaining a situation; that I had no friends in the world, and that I had travelled from a distant part of the country; but I was cautious enough, not to reveal the particulars of my adventures with the gipsies. My account seemed to afford them a considerable deal of gratification, and they exchanged significant looks with one another, which I did not at all like. At length the whole of the other lodgers had gradually retired to their respective mattresses, and my companions having drank all their beer, and smoked out their tobacco, stretched themselves at full length on the floor, yawned two or three times, and fell off to sleep also. I felt tired and sleepy, but my fears kept me awake, and I sat musing in my chair, cogitating on the singularity of my fate, and the gloominess of my present prospects; while the loud snoring of the lodgers, alone disturbed the death-like stillness of this miserable abode. At length the light which had long be faintly glimmering in the lamp, went out entirely, and the place was involved in complete darkness. I could hear the wind whistling without, and piercing gusts howled in at several of the broken squares of glass, which rattled in the frames of the only window in the room. I felt cold, and wretched, and the horrors of my fate seemed to accumulate round me. What would I have given to have been out of that horrid place, and from the the company into which I had so unfortunately fallen. With the futile hope of still being able to make my escape, I went to the door of the apartment, for a moment entertaining an idea that Mrs. Botts, might have forgotten to fasten it when she brought the young men's beer; but I soon found how fallacious was this hope, it was quite fast. I listened at it, but could not hear a sound, and cheerless, heartless, and tired I returned to my chair, and not liking to lay down on the filthy mattresses, and by the side of the still more filthy persons who inhabited them, completely overcome and tired, I at last dropt off to sleep. I was so fatigued with travelling, that I slept soundly, and did not awake, until the noise of the cadgers aroused me, when I found it was day-light, that many of the persons had quitted the room, and that others were preparing to follow their example. My first thought was about my money, and putting my hand down to my stocking, I felt the the bag there all safe.

"Bill Stokes, and Georgy Miles which I had understood were the names of the two prepossessing young gentlemen who had taken such a deep interest in my affairs on the previous night, had already escaped from the bondage of sleep, and observed my action:—

" 'Hollo, young man,' exclaimed Bill, 'vhy how your leg's svell'd; I s'pose you've met with an accident in valkin'!'

"This question confused me, but glad of the opinion Bill had expressed, I thought it best to let him entertain the same idea, therefore declared that I had stumbled over a stone on the road, and injured my ancle.

"Bill Stokes, however, was not to be easily deceived as I very soon found out; he expressed great pity at my accident, and hoped that I would not be so foolish as to neglect doing something to it, or I might be a cripple all my life through it. I thanked him for his advice, and said I would seek a remedy for it as soon as I went out. This I thought would stop all further questions, but I was mistaken.

" 'It does seem werry much svelled tho',' observed Bill, 'let me look at it, for I had a bad pin myself vonce, and I knows a little how to act vith them here

sort of things; jist pull down yer stocking and let's have a look at it!'

"My confusion at this moment must have betrayed me; for Bill and Georgy winked at one another, in silent approval of their sagacity, while I stammered forth a lame excuse, and held tight hold of my stocking, pushing away the hands of Bill, who prepared to pull it down without any further ceremony.

" 'Vy, vot's the cove afeard on,' said the worthy Georgy; 'he holds his pin as tight as if it vos a gold von and ve vos a goin' to rob him on it!'

"While Georgy was making use of these observation, Bill had proceeded by main force to tear my stocking down, and oh, conceive my agitation, my grief, when he pulled forth my treasured bag, and shaking it with a laugh at his companion, exclaimed:—

" 'Here's a rummy svellin' Georgy!'

" 'Vy it's blunt, arnt it?' said the gentleman to whom the former exclamation had been addressed.

" 'To be sure it is,' replied Mr. Stokes, turning out the whole of the contents of the bag into his hand, and counting them over with evident satisfaction;—'Seven half *bulls*!—Vell, vhat a artful cove to say he had no ochre!'

" 'Oh, do not rob me of my money,' I exclaimed with tears in my eyes, and clasping my hands in agony at the prospect of my being left pennyless; 'I will freely give you part of it, but if you take it all, I shall starve in a place where I am a stranger, and have not a single friend!'

"My pathetic appeal was received with a very complacent grin both by Mr. Stokes and his friend, and the former gentleman was proceeding without any further ceremony to consign the money to his own pocket, when I again implored them to have compassion on me.

" 'Valker!'' replied Mr. Miles, giving more definitive expression to his sentiments, by working an imaginary telegraph on his nose with his thumb and four fingers. 'How green you are, arnt yer? It's no go, you vont gammon us, my fine feller; no doubt you nibbled this here from some von, and as a matter of course ve havin' only found it, have a much greater right to it than you!'

"This original sort of logic, I was not prepared to contradict, and I could only reply to it, by asserting my innocence of dishonesty, and once more soliciting them to restore me part, if not the whole of the money. It may be imagined that it was a very useless attempt to seek to move the pity of those beings who had never heard of such a sentiment, but I succeeded in one way, as you will hear, only I cannot undertake to say whether pity had any thing do with the business; a sudden thought seemed to dart across the ponderous brain of Mr. Stokes, and returning the money to the bag, he drew his friend aside, and held a brief conversation with him in an under tone of voice, and whatever the nature of it might be, certain it is that it ultimately gained the approving nod of Mr. Miles, who by the grin that overspread his features, seemed remarkably well pleased with the idea, which had emanated from the prolific brain of Mr. Stokes. Their secret conference being ended, Mr. Stokes drew me aside, and said in a tone of voice which could not be overheard by any of the other individuals in the room, he thus addressed me:

"'It's no use young feller, your trying to come the old soldier over us, because yer see ve happen to be too vide avake; it may be all werry vell your begammonin' some people as how yer get this here blunt honestly, but ve are down, asides, how is a poor friendless cove, as you says yer are, to get all this here tin; it von't do; there's not a doubt but you've boned it from some vun, and if I liked I could keep it myself, or else give yer up to th' traps, and then you'd be sent off to quod and lagged to a certainty! But as I doesn't vant to be hard vith yer, I'll tell yer vot I'll do; I'll give yer all the tip back again, but you must go vith me an' Georgy to day, an' stan' Sam for all ve has; yer needn't be afeard to trust yerself vith us, ve are werry 'spectable chaps, I can tell yer. Besides, you say as how yer vants a situation, and if you come vith us, ve'll put yer into summat as vill make your fortin'! Come, vot d'yer say?—Yer'll never have sich a chance agin, an' if yer don't take it, vy th' blunt's mine!'

"This proposal I at first thought would be worse than the loss of my money, for what dangers might I not be led into in the society of two such fellows as Messrs. Stokes and Miles; but when I thought upon the former individual's threats to give me into custody on a charge of robbery, my fears overcame me; besides, I reflected, there might be a chance of my escaping from the wretches after we had got into the street; and without money, what could I do?—I therefore determined to accede to Mr. Stokes's proposal, and signified the same to him.

"'You're no flat for agreeing,' observed Bill, 'but mind yer, my cove, no attempting to sneak off; it von't do to try it on, I can tell yer!'

"With this precaution, he returned me the money, and we prepared to leave the house. Upon descending the stairs, I recollected the half crown I had left in the hands of the *worthy* Mrs. Botts on the previous evening, and accordingly hastened into the place that lady dignified with the name of a parlour, to request my change.

" I found the worthy proprietress of this very noted snoozing ken, seated upon the knee of one of the gentlemen who had been in her society on the preceeding evening, and whose affections seemed to be very equally divided between her lover and a rump steak and a plentiful supply of potatoes which were smoking on the table before them, and was intended for a light breakfast. Upon my entrance she did not seem by any means abashed, and prudently retained her seat on the lap of the very interesting looking male who supported her.

"'Vell, my dear,' exclaimed Mrs. Botts, in her most insinuating style, 'How did yer like yer bed; I hope yer slept vell; but I'm sure yer must, for though I say it vot shouldn't say it, my beds is the best, and my lodgin's is the most respectablist in London; yer vouldn't find sich accommodation any vhere else, no not even in *Saffron Hill*, for all it's reckon'd th' most fash'nable part of the whole of this great *'trop'lis*, by al those who 'onner me with their company!'

"Notwithstanding this apparent impartial critique upon her establishment, I could have given a very different opinion, had I not thought that a silent assent to Mrs. Botts' eulogiums would probably be the most prudent on that occasion.

"'Ah,' resumed Mrs. Botts, as well as she could, considering that she had just deposited about a quarter of a pound of the steak, and a large kidney potatoe, in her mouth; 'I thought as how yer'd like yer lodgin's, so I s'pose you'll come here agin; I know yer can't get a better crib. Yer see, I keeps it so select an' comfortable, and that's more than yer vould find many o' th' houses in London, I can tell yer. London's a werry vicked place, an' a young man like you should be werry cautious into whose care he puts himself; for, though I say it that shouldn't say it, there's not many vomen in the vorld like Mrs. Botts!'

"With a charitable regard for my fellow creatures, I thoroughly credited the last observation of the *respectable* Mrs. Botts; but, anxious to get away from this abominable den, I made no reply to what she had said, but simply requested that she would be so kind as to give me the two shillings that were due to me from the half-crown I had given her on the previous evening. No sooner had I made the demand, than a change took place in the countenance of the amiable Mrs. Botts of the most extraordinary nature; she stared at me with well assumed astonishment and incredulity, and then exclaimed:

" ' Mercy on me, why the child must be dreaming, or else he's an artful young rogue; two shillin's, vhy, he knows werry vell, and so does this gentleman here, that he said he had only a sixpence in the vorld, and that he gave me, and now he vants to gammon that he gave a half-bull! Vell, I never !'

" It was very evident I was duped out of my money, by the *honest* Mrs Botts, and as it was not likely that I should get any satisfaction from such individuals, and being also fearful that I might exasperate them to ill-treat me; I made as plausible an apology as I could, and observed that I must have been mistaken. With this apology, after several affirmations of her strict integrity from Mrs. Botts, was finally accepted, and in company with Messrs. Stokes and Miles, I quitted the Cadger's Snoozing Ken.

" It was near twelve o'clock in the noon, and the clamour of business was at its utmost pitch, all was bustle and confusion. My companions kept close by my side, and I observed that they nodded familiarly to several males and females of questionable appearance, in our progress through the streets, and to every one of the proprietors of those shops in which so many silk handkerchiefs are always exposed for sale. My thoughts were none of the most agreeable nature you may be assured, and I viewed the continual changing novelty with an indifference that nothing but my critical situation could have occasioned me to feel. As for my companions, they amused themselves at times by whistling, at others by singing, and by occasional passing observations on the objects which engaged their attention as we walked along. I looked wistfully up every street we passed, and several times felt half inclined to run, but then the threats of Bill Stokes recurred to my memory, and I abandoned all idea of it, giving myself up entirely to fate. I racked my brain in vain to find something that could afford me the least idea of where the fellows intended to take me.

and what they could mean by the *situation* they had promised to get me; but my thoughts were all fruitless and I gave up the attempt in despair. We walked along Holborn, until we arrived at a dirty looking public house, into which Bill Stokes beckoned me and his companion, at the same time observing that his thorux was very dry, and therefore he thought a drop of something reviving would not at all be ill-timed or unacceptable. In this opinion of course, Mr. Miles coincided, and Bill walking up to the bar, gave the necessary order for what he wanted, which was quickly complied with in the shape of half a pint of gin, for which an immediate demand was made upon my bag. Messrs. Stokes and Miles having both swallowed a large glass-full of the beverage with all the adriotness of the most skilful practitioners, filled a glass and handed it to me; I refused it, upon which Mr. Stokes and his friend indulged in a laugh of the most ineffable contempt.

" ' What a yokel!' exclaimed the former personage, ' he doesn't know vot's good for him !'

" And to prove the superiority of his judgment over mine, he gulped down the contents of the glass, and what was left in the measure with remarkable ease and condescension. We then issued from the public house and resumed our peregrinations.

" The yawning of some of the learned members of *The Cadgers' Society*, now warned *Scapegrace Jack*, that the lateness of the hour would prevent the possibility of his concluding his important autobiography that night; he therefore paused, and after some trifling proceedings which it is not worth while to mention here, the club as usual was dissolved till the next evening, when they re-assembled at an early hour, and in the same numerous manner that they had done ever since the commencement of Jack's recital of his wonderful adventures. Attention having been obtained, the narrator resumed his narrative as follows :

" I am afraid gentlemen, that I have intruded longer upon your time than the interest of my story will warrant, but I have only a few more remarkable incidents to relate to you, and my tale is ended.

"We crossed the road into Chancery Lane, and pursued our way into Fleet Street, and so on till we arrived at the ancient city of Westminster, and in that, one of its most fashionable places, y'clept Tothill Street! In this street my companions recognised several individuals of the ragged and dirty order, and one or two young *ladies* whose respectable professions were evident from the happy familiarity of their manners. We passed through Tothill Street, and entered the Broadway, passing hastily along, amid the bustle and confusion of drunken soldiers, and importunate costermongers. I now ventured to inquire of my companions for the first time, whither we were going.

"'Not much farther,' replied Bill Stokes, 'I'm getting rather peckish, an' so I think th' best thing we can do is to go into a *ho-tell* an' blow our kites out!'

"This suggestion received an aproving smile from Georgy Miles, and we hurried on until we arrived at those very classic regions known as the Almoury.

"Bill Stokes and Georgy Miles," continued Jack, "stood contemplating the unprepossessing edibles, that were displayed in the shop window of this establishment for a few seconds, and after turning their glances first upon some pease pudding in a broken dish, which seemed to be in their estimation of a very tempting quality, and then removing them to some dingy looking square pieces in another dish, which Bill designated 'plum duff,' they finally turned them upon a bill in the window, which stated that leg of beef soup might be obtained inside at any hour of the day; and this bill seeming to express the dish most in unison with their palates on that occasion, they signified their intention to me of entering the *hotel*. Of course I knew it would be useless to offer any objection to this proposition; besides, I myself felt rather hungry, and doubted not but that I should be able to devour some of the fare, although it did not look very savoury.

"Accordingly, in we walked, and seating ourselves in a box adjoining one in which three young *ladies* and two gentlemen, with corkscrew like ringlets flowing down their cheeks, had ensconced themselves, Bill Stokes, who took upon himself the important office of spokesman upon all occasions, ordered in 'three *threes* and taters,' which speedily made their appearance smoking hot, and were immediately pounced upon by my companions with a most acute appetite!

"It is quite unnecessary for me to detain you here by giving any kind of detail of the place or '*Hotel*,' in which we now were, as you must all be thoroughly acquainted with these matters, it is quite enough for me to apprize you that the knives and forks were chained to the table, with all that sensible precaution that it is found necessary to adopt in the victualling departments of our highly respectable fraternity, and also that a bill was very conspicuously displayed in the shop, with the usual announcement upon it of, "To *perwent* mistakes, all wittuls must be tipt for on delivery!"

"After I had managed with infinite difficulty to digest one basin full of what was christened leg of beef soup, and my companions had in the same space of time very coolly put out of sight four basins each, and as many 'goes' of potatoes, my fast diminishing bank stock being once more taxed to settle the demand, we arose and departed. I cannot at this distance of time enter into a precise history of our afternoon's rambles on that memorable occasion; it is sufficient to say that as the evening approached I found myself only in the possession of one half crown, Bill Stokes and Georgy Miles having kindly spent the remainder for me in sundry outlays for 'Shag,' and the 'Elixir of Life;' and to add to the pleasures of their society, they gave evident symptoms of having taken just enough of the latter article to make them very jolly, and at the same time very ferocious. I several times attempted to escape from them, but all my efforts were ineffectual, and at length the two *worthy* individuals who held me in their custody, ventured to threaten me with the most summary and severe punishment, if I attempted to decamp again. I looked around me with the vain hope of seeing some passengers to whom I might appeal, and who would intercede in my behalf; but as we were in the lowest part of Westminster, the only countenances I beheld were as disgusting and reckless as those that were owned by Mr. Stokes and his colleague. Wound up to a pitch of misery almost indescribable as I reflected upon the perverseness of my fate, which from infancy had seemed to lavish nothing but trouble upon my head, and to make me the very football of my fellow creatures, I worked myself into such a state of mind that I began to care little what might become of me; I imagined that some accursed spell was upon me, and that however I might strive by the rectitude of my conduct, to merit a better fate, infamy and beggary was ordained for me, and that I might as well therefore, quietly resign myself to a fate that I could not controul, as by any futile opposition seek to aggravate it. I firmly believe that it was these reflections that finally made my fortune, for had they not have occurred to me, I should have undoubtedly have continued to refuse to listen to the advice of those who knew better than myself, and thus have never arrived at that eminence in my *profession* which has accumulated me all the fortune I now possess. I reflected upon all the incidents of my short life, and the more I thought upon them, the more convinced I became that it was my fate to be a vagabond. I was born of a villain; and temporary as had been my correspondence with virtue and happiness, I was doomed to be discarded even by them; death first robbed me of the best of mothers; and the same power deprived me of one of the most generous of benefactors; I was then driven upon the world! and almost immediately thrown into the power of the gipsies, from whom I was transferred to my present respectable companions, whose characters I deemed very little better, if any, than the ferocious ruffians from whom I had escaped, and made my way to London. All these reflections had a very strange effect upon me, and I felt something like recklessness overpowering all my other senti-

ments. I know the-would-be virtuous who may read these sentiments at any future period, will shrug up their shoulders, and exclaim, ' Oh, you should have kept honest, and not weakly have suffered temptation to subdue your good qualities !' Very good; honesty may be all very well for those to preach who have been born to wealth plundered by their ancestors; but I can vouch for the truth of the statement, when I say to those who are born to poverty, honesty is at best a buggaboo, a kind of Poor Law Commissioner under the present admirable order of the bill, whose business 'tis to gripe the bowels of those unfortunates who seek his aid, and to sport it in the guise of charity, at the same time he deals out slow murder to all who have the accursed ill-fortune to apply to him, But these observations will shew the state of my mind at the time, and give some reason for my becoming that singular character that afterwards obtained for me the cognomen of 'Scapegrace Jack.'

" By the time night approached, I had so freely indulged in the thoughts I have just quoted, that I even ventured to treat my companions with more complaisance than they had hitherto obtained from me; a circumstance which seemed to afford them infinate pleasure, and they exchanged looks between each other, which I easily having interpreted as follows: —" He'll do in time." So far in fact had my ideas altered upon material points, that I assented to a proposition made by Bill Stokes, namely, that we should go into an adjacent shop, and treat ourselves to another small drain of that they had already so liberally partaken of, and with more skill than might have been expected from my youth and inexperience, I swallowed a glass of what my companions termed the most " precious stuff," but which, I must acknowledge was, in my opinion, any thing but delicious. My companions perceiving that I had become so pleasant and compliant, informed me that my fortune was made since I had met with them, and that they were now about to introduce me to some of the first fellows that ever existed; *gentlemen* who lived as they pleased, and cared something considerablv more insignificant than a d—n for any body; they also added that they did not fear but that if I was careful it would be the best thing that ever happened to me, and far preferable to the spooney life I had wished to live. Being somewhat exhilarated by the effects of the gin, I listened to these observations with much satisfaction, and expressed to them my willingness to put myself entirely under their guidance. Messrs. Stokes and Miles again expressed their approval of my acquiescence, and as it was now getting late, they each of them took one of my arms, and proceeded to conduct me up several dark lanes, muddy and narrow streets, and short and ill-lighted courts and alleys, until I found we were in the same street in which the 'Hotel' was situated where we had partaken of our repast. We proceeded on our way until we arrived at what appeared to be a very miserable chandlers shop, and one of the most old fashioned houses in the street. The windows was embellished with the commonest blue and notted glass, which was, in addition to its natural dimness, thickly coated with dirt, which buried what few miserable articles that were meant to be exposed for sale, in complete obscurity. There were two or three broken steps to ascend to the door of the shop, which was one of those ancient, clumsily carved ones that are still to be seen in some of the low streets of the metropolis.

"'You must not say any thin' as ve go along;' observed Bill Stokes to me, as him and Georgy proceeded to ascend the steps, and dragged me after them. I nodded my assent to this caution, and we entered the shop. Behind the counter was a little bony, grizly, haggish looking old woman; who was smoking a short pipe when we entered, and upon seeing us, took it from her lips for a minute, and fixed her eyes scrutinizingly upon me, afterwards turning towards my companions with a look of inquiry.

"'All right, mother Munns!' said Bill Stokes, passing on to a back door, which was behind the counter, and opened into a short yard. The old woman merely nodded her head at this, as if she was satisfied, and resumed her seat and her pipe. At the back of this yard were some large wooden premises which had the appearance of work-shops. Bill Stokes advanced with me towards a door at which he gave three distinct knocks, and after a pause he was answered by a gruff voice from within, who demanded who was there?

"'All right Jim, it's me and Georgy!' replied the individual to whom the question was addressed.

"'Oh,' briefly responded the person on the other side of the door, and immediately afterwards two or three bolts were withdrawn, and the door slowly opened, disclosing a dark passage and a dirty porter with a lamp in his hand.

"'Are the kids all there?' inquired Mr. Stokes.

"'Yes, they're all in th' ken!' replied the person who had opened the door.

"'It's all right then!' remarked Bill, 'you can bolt the door agin, and go first vith the lamp, for it's precious dark here.'

Jim obeyed the orders of Mr. Stokes without saying a word, and we traversed the full extent of this passage which was not a short one, and ascended a ladder at the extremity, which conducted us to a sort of leads covered over. Upon reaching this place, the sound of many voices burst upon my ears, seemingly excited by the very height of mirth and revelry; and I could distinguish a peculiar set of oaths at intervals which gave me no very high opinion of the parties to whom I was about to be introduced. I recollected the caution of Bill, however, and did not venture to make any observation; although the mystery with which every thing had hitherto been conducted excited the utmost interest and curiosity in my mind. There was something altogether so very romantic in the adventure, that it was a source rather of amusement to me than terror, and I was completely on the tiptoe of expectation, from which neither of my companions seemed inclined to arouse me for the present. We passed across these leads, and opening another door had evidently entered a house that had no connexion with the chandler's shop, although they had been made to communicate with each other.

"The voices of the company that was assembled in some portion of the building, now could be heard more distinct; rude songs, boisterous acclamations, loud peals of laughter, and indecent oaths were mingled strangely together, and as I listened to them, and thought of the mysterious manner in which I had been conveyed thither, I felt my old fears gradually stealing over me, and I would gladly have been in the street again, and at liberty. My companions doubtless guessed the thoughts that were passing in my mind, for I observed them wink at one another, and then they pulled me hastily after them into the passage to which the door led, which closed with a loud slam after us. We now found ourselves on a very old fashioned staircase, which was very wide and lofty. By the clearness of the sounds that had so lately alarmed me, it was evident we were not far from where the parties were carousing, and that it was to them we were going. We began to ascend the staircase, and after making our way up two flights we stopped at a door, which evidently opened into the apartment in which the people were so merry.

"'Tip the spell?' observed Mr. Stokes addressing himself mysteriously to our conductor. Jim advanced to the door, which seemed to be bolted inside, and gave three significant knocks on it. A dead silence from within the room immediately followed, and no one would now have supposed it to be inhabited. At last a hoarse voice from within whispered through the key-hole and asked who was there; to which Jim made answer by giving utterance to some expression which I cannot now recollect, but which I afterwards understood was the secret watch-word chozen for the night; the following moment the door was thrown back on its hinges, my companions laid hold of me tightly one by each arm, and led me to the centre of the room; I looked round with astonishment and stuperfaction at the remarkable scene that was revealed to me, and I am certain you will not be surprised at my amazement when I inform you that I was in the far famed *Beggar's haunt*, which at that time was established in the Almoury, and conducted so secretly, that characters of all descriptions might find a safe retreat therein, without any fear of detection unless it was by one of the visitors to this ken peaching, a thing that not one was ever known to be guilty of. You are aware, my friends, that there are at the present day a number of similar places, both in Westminister, Whitechapel, Seven Dials, and Saint Giles'; but they none of them have been enabled to attain that perfection with which they were conducted in the days I am speaking of. The place I am speaking of, was erected at the back of the premises belonging entirely to one man, and the entrances to it were through shops in the front streets, which to prevent suspicion, made a semblance of dealing in various articles, such as old clothes, fish, &c. The shops that I have described as looking like work-shops, were used for various purposes, namely *Fences, Private Stills, Coining,* and various other equally legal doings.

"I fear I shall fail most wofully in attempting any thing like an accurate description of the *haunt* and the company who were in it assembled. It was an immense long room well lighted, and with a good fire in it at each end. It was parted off into different compartments something like a tap-room, with a table to each, at which were chummed beggars of various grades both male and female, youthful and aged;—decrepid and sound, dirty and respectable, each partaking of what they liked best, both in the eatable and drinkable way, but every one having a most ample supply. Others were amusing themselves with various games, such as cards, dominoes, *Shove half-penny, Ring the Bull, Cod'em,* and several other equally agreeable and *fashionable* sports, which I cannot recollect at the present moment but with which you are all equally well acquainted as myself. Every one of them seemed remarkably happy, particularly a party or two of boys, the eldest evidently not more than fifteen years of age, who had each got a female about their own age, and were smoking short pipes with an ease and energy that plainly showed, although young in point of age, they were old practitioners. There were a couple of fowls roasting before the fire, and rump steaks were hissing on the gridiron above it. The place had all the appearance of the low tap-room of an old fashioned public house, and so any one would have taken it to be from the large casks of spirits it contained, the whole of which were, however, manufactured in the way I have mentioned, in defiance of the Revenue.

"No sooner had we entered this curious haunt, than the whole of the persons arose and fixed their gaze upon me, from which I shrank back in confusion; then seeing in whose care I was, they all shouted together several slang terms, which signified that another green one was added to their noble fraternity. All my former fears returned upon beholding the singular and very unprepossessing individuals to whom I was introduced, which were not at all diminished upon hearing the beggars pass very curious observations upon my personal appearance and giving various opinions as to the uses I was most qualified to be put; some contending that I was almost too big for an orphan child; and others declaring that my pale countenance and thin figure would do excellent to gammon a poor starved lad!—Some said that if I could be initiated into the art of fit shamming, I should make many a person's fortune, others gave it as their sage opinion that I might do a deal with a broom; while one dark man, attired in a velveteen kind of shooting jacket, a white silk hat, corded knee unmentionables, worsted stockings and ankle boots, after taking a minute survey of my figure, and examining my hands with great care, gave it as his decided opinion, that I should make a capital '*diver*' because my '*mawleys*' were so light.

"While these various opinions had been spoken freely about, Bill Stokes leaving me under the especial care of Georgy Miles, had been buried in profound conversation with a tall and rather respectable looking man, who was attending to one of the fowls, and I had very good reason to suppose from the manner in which they directed their glances, and pointed towards me, that I was the subject of their conversation

At length the fowl being done, and Mr. Stokes and the stranger having probably come to some satisfactory conclusion upon the subject they were conversing about, the former beckoned to Georgy, who without any more invitation, proceeded to obey the summons, desiring me to walk with him.

"The fowl having been taken from the fire, was borne by the individual to whom Bill had been talking, to a box at which a female about thirty, with an infant at her breast was seated; and a man who was the waiter to the place, although he carried any thing but the look of a waiter in his appearance, attended a motion of the respectable looking man, who desired him to provide him with plates, knives and forks, and all the necessary utensils for eating. The man obeyed, and in the meantime, the man who appeared to be the woman's husband, seated himself by her side, and Bill Stokes and Georgy Miles, seating me in between them, took their places on the other.

"'Th' kid looks afeared,' observed Mr. Stokes, addressing himself to the respectable looking man, and alluding to me.

"'Well, there is nothing surprising in that;' remarked the man, 'but you have no occasion to feel alarmed, my lad,' he continued, looking rather kindly upon me, 'nobody here shall harm you, I,ll take good care of that!'

"The mild manners, and difference of the appearance of the man altogether to any of the rest of the persons who were in the room, prepossessed me in his favour, and much pleased to find at at least one who seemed likely to commiserate with me, I could not help in a very civil manner thanking him for his kindness; whereupon Messrs. Stokes and Miles indulged in a mutual laugh, and exchanged sundry winks with one another, which were, however speedily checked by a frown from the proprietor of the roast fowl.

"The fowl and all the necessary appurtenances being duly arranged on the table, we all prepared to play an active part in its dissection, I being encouraged to eat, by the attention which the respectable looking man paid me, and it was not long before the supper vanished from the table, as did also several pots of beer, of which I was persuaded to drink heartily. The woman, whom I now understood was really the partner of the respectable looking man, seemed to eye me with as much interest and kindness as her husband, and I confess, what with the effects of this, of the supper I had eaten, the porter I had drank, I began to feel not altogether dissatisfied. Messrs. Stokes and Miles, having amused themselves as long as they felt inclined with conversing along with the respectable looking man, whom they designated Bunckey, and drank as much of the porter as they thought proper, re-filled their pipes, and hastened to join a party of ragged looking beings at the other end of the room, who were dancing to the music of another gentleman in a short fustian jacket, who was whistling most melodiously, and giving a curious sort of accompaniament by hammering with the palms of his hands and his elbows on the table.

" In these Terpsichorean amusements the whole of the remainder of the motley guests shortly joined, and I was left to the society of my new companions.

" Not long had they gone, and Mr. Bunckey had satisfied himself by putting innumerable questions to me, the whole of which I answered without hesitation, when I felt a strange and unaccountable drowsiness stealing over my senses, which I vainly endeavoured to shake off. What could occasion this, I at that time was of course not prepared to form any conjecture of; but I have not the slightest reason to doubt, that the beer was drugged, as we had two pots up at a time, and I now remember very well, that Messrs. Stokes and Miles always monopolized one particular pot to themselves, while Mr. Bunckey and his wife drank out of the same pot as myself, and naver failed when it came to my turn, to urge me to drink deep, for that t would do me good ; although at the same time I could not help remarking that Mr. and Mrs. Bunckey were particularly modest in their own libations.

" However, it is not to be supposed, that simple as I then was, I could have any suspicion of what was really going on, and I consequently became an easy victim. Mr. Bunckey still kept urging me to drink deep, and as I became more stupified, I knew not scarcely what I was doing, so therefore complied with his requests to the very letter; until the effects of the strong soperofic that had been mixed in the beer overpowered me, and I became insensible to all around me.

" When I recovered my senses, the place I found myself in, was so different to the curious scene I had last been in, that I could scarcely credit my eye-sight. I was lying upon an extremely clean bed, in a carpeted apartment, very handsomely furnished, and with a cheerful fire blazing in it. The sun was streaming powerfully into the room, in spite of the long blinds with which the windows were shaded, and I therefore imagined, (for I in a moment recollected the previous night's adventures,) that I must have slept for many hours. But where could I be ?—To what place had I been transported, so widely different from the one I had last been in ?—And what could be the meaning of it all ?—I rubbed my eyes, and raising myself on my elbow, looked with astonishment around the chamber. A female form then attracted my attention, seated at the further end of the apartment attentively perusing a book. As I coughed slightly two or three times, it aroused her, and advancing immediately towards me, I recognized in the features and person of the woman, those of my previous night's acquaintance, namely Mrs. Bunckey !

" Upon observing my astonishment, she attempted to appease the remarks I seemed inclined to make, but she could not restrain the expression of my astonishment.

" ' Where am I ?'—I exclaimed, ' and for what purpose am I brought hither ?— Where is Mr. Stokes, and what is become of his companion, Georgy Miles ?

" ' Hush, hush, my dear !' said Mrs. Bunckey in a very kind tone of voice, ' you shall know every thing bye and bye ; but at present you had better try to compose yourself to sleep, and I will call you when dinner's ready. Does your head ache, my love ?'

POSTHUMOUS PAPERS

OF THE

CADGERS' CLUB.

" I replied in the affirmative, but I only accounted for it by having drank too much on the previous night, and being unused to take any sort of drink before.

" ' Very well, my dear,' observed Mrs. Bunckey, ' a little sleep will refresh you so; so do try and compose yourself, that's a good boy!'

" With these words, without giving me time to make any reply, Mrs. Bunckey bounded out of the room almost imperceptibly, and, in spite of my surprise, I did indeed fall into another deep sleep, from which I did not awaken for many hours afterwards.

" I now heard a slight noise below,

No. 10.

and got out of bed and went to the room door, which was quite fast. I then put my ear to the keyhole, and tried to catch the words that were articulated by many voices altogether below, but that I found to be impossible; so I returned to the bed, and made up my mind to await patiently the result of this curious adventure. Presently afterwards I heard a footstep upon the stairs, and then the room door was unlocked, and Mrs. Bunckey again presented herself before me.

" Seeing that I was awake, she once more inquired affectionately after my health; and upon my replying that my head was much better, she informed me that I might get up, and accompany her down stairs to dinner. With this request I lost no time in complying, and was very speedily equipped.

"I found no one but Mr. Bunckey in the parlour of my new residence, which was furnished with the same degree of neatness, and even elegance, as the one in which I had been reposing. Mr. Bunckey received me with much kindness, and I confess that his manner completely won my good opinion. Little did I suspect at that time that he was the adept at dissimulation and roguery which I very soon discovered afterwards. He was, in fact, one of the most accomplished of the cadging fraturnity, and to him I am indebted for nearly all those *brilliant* accomplishments which have been the means of raising me to such a pre-eminence in my profession.

"There was a very comfortable repast prepared for me, which I partook of with an excellent appetite, my mind being more composed than it had been for some time. During this meal, Mr. Bunckey inquired, with much apparent solicitude, into my history, which I unfolded to him without any attempt at concealment, and at the conclusion he embraced me with much fatherly affection, called me his son, and promised me, if I behaved myself, he would be a protector to me, and look out for some means by which I could get my future living. I thanked him very much for his kindness, and promised to do all in my power to render myself worthy of his benevolence. My behaviour seemed to afford both Mr. and Mrs. Bunckey considerable satisfaction, and the remainder of that day was passed without any particular occurrence worthy of detailing.

"It would be a fruitless occupation of your time, which I have already so long intruded upon, were I to relate minutely all the deep-laid stratagems that the artful Mr. Bunckey and his worthy partner put in practice to seduce me into their course of life, and to make a property of me, as they had done many others. I soon discovered, as I dare say you have all guessed by this time, the real characters and professions of my protectors. They were wholesale traffickers in the cultivation of the talents of juvenile outcasts. The house in which I first found myself was their *private* residence, where they lived in the greatest luxury, upon the fruits of their nefarious practices, unsuspected and unmolested. They kept in their employ a great number of cadgers of all descriptions, whom they boarded and lodged at a wretched dog-hole in the beautiful neighbourhood of Wentworth-street, Whitechapel, to which I was very shortly afterwards introduced. Beggars and vagrants of every description, age, and grade, were in their employ, being allowed by them a weekly stipend for their labours, and provided with lush, victuals, and other enticing luxuries in abundance, on the condition of their delivering to them the receipts of their daily avocations. If a poor wretch was starving and driven to desperation, he or she had only to apply to Mr. Bunckey, through the means of his agents, of whom he employed several in various parts of the metropolis, and they were soon initiated into the particular branches of the trade for which they seemed best qualified, and supplied with the means of procuring a *decent* living. Every species of vice was encouraged, practised, and taught, by the *amiable* Mr. Bunckey, and so great was his power over mendicants and prigs of all descriptions, that they dared not attempt to deceive him. He was well acquainted with all the officers, whom he paid handsomely to keep his secrets, and therefore set the law at defiance. If any of his servants were treacherous, they were sure of punishment, for they were immediately given into the care of one of the officers, who never failed to trump up such cases against them as always secured them either transportation or imprisonment, according as the *merits* or demerits of the case demanded; and if they in retaliation attempted to stigmatise the character of Mr. Bunckey, he had always plenty of apparently respectable witnesses ready to come forward to exonerate his character, and generally escaped with a compliment from the magistrate, and the usual addenda that he left the office without the slightest blemish on his conduct. Knowing the utter fruitlessness of such proceedings,

Mr. Bunckey was seldom troubled, and his victims very seldom were disobedient to his will. At his den in Wentworth-street, he kept a private fence, and was always ready to ease the adventurous of their 'swag' upon the most liberal terms. He had a vast number of juveniles in his employ, who followed various branches of begging and thieving, for the whole of which accomplishments they were indebted to Mr. Bunckey's *admirable* instructions, and whose anger they dreaded as much as the unhappy slave dreads his ferocious driver.

"Neither was Mrs. Bunckey an indolent woman, for she conducted a large brothel at the west end of the town, and her days were passed at the different coach-offices, ready to pounce upon the simple country girl, and trepan her into her designs. She was not less successful than her husband by these manœuvres, and many were the poor girls who had to date their ruin from this clever pander in female prostitution. It may easily be imagined that these various and profitable avocations could not fail to make Mr. and Mrs. Bunckey very rich: and being both really accomplished and intelligent people, and living in such splendour at their *private* residence, it is no wonder that their society was courted by the most respectable individuals, and it was no uncommon thing for them both to be invited to the party of a gentleman who, probably, but a day or two before had been robbed or duped by their instructions and their *domestics*.

"I have before stated at some length my sentiments previous to entering the *Beggar's Haunt*, and it will not therefore be a matter of surprise, that those ideas were speedily cultivated and encouraged with avidity by my new benefactor, who gave me such daily lessons in the art of despising the opinion of the world, and shewed me the advantages of pursuing a jovial, adventurous, don't-care sort of life, over the folly of running after what he designated the *ignis fatuus*, honesty, that I finally laughed at my former squeamishness, and agreed without a murmur to follow the advice of Mr. Bunckey to the very letter. This triumph over my scruples was hailed by the *vagrant proprietor*, with the most undisguised delight, and a consultation was held upon the most probable branch for me to adopt, and in which I was calculated best to *shine!* This was found to be no easy task, for being put to the test, it was discovered that I had such a versatility of talents, that it was a matter of extreme doubt, in which I should prove most successful.

"Misery had endowed me with many natural accomplishments, which being now called into action as a means of existence, seemed likely to afford me a very rich harvest. For instance, it was no matter of difficulty for me to assume a most woe-begone and pitiful expression of countenance, since having experienced nothing else but grief from my infancy, my visage had become pliable to that sort of assumption by habit. I could cry with the greatest of ease, for I had been so used to tears, that I had a constant reservoir in my head which I could draw from whenever I thought proper. As for shamming fits, it was soon evident, that I was a perfect adept in that difficult and nice point of vagrancy.

"My qualifications for my new mode of life, being thus made apparent, the time was fixed for me to make a trial of my skill in public, and I was accordingly fully attired after the most approved plan of misery, and hastened, followed at a distance by Mr. Bunckey, to a large public thoroughfare in the neighbourhood of Portman Square, where I took up my station with a label on my breast which informed the public that I was a poor orphan boy, who was starving. Mr. Bunckey stood within sight to watch how I performed my part, and to prevent my escaping, if I had entertained such a design, and it was really surprising, considering it being my first effort, how well I performed my task. I put on a countenance that would even have put the much talked of raw-head and bloody bones to the blush; and I shook every limb, (partly I own with real apprehension,) just as though every joint of my frame was unhinged, and I was on the point of expiring. My success was as great as it was sudden; my wretched appearance excited the compassion of almost every one that passed, and money teemed into my pocket with most gratifying rapidity. I was a little fearful at times of receiving a lodging in the workhouse by the over zealous sympathy of some of the passengers, who suggested the propriety of my being taken to some place of shelter to prevent me expiring in the street. At such times, however, Mr. Bunckey who kept a vigilant look out, always stepped up, and by pretending to take compassion on me, and bidding me follow him to an asylum, always succeeded in removing me safely out of the way, until the too-officious people had dispersed. The success of my first day's vagrancy was declared by Mr. Bunckey to have been quite unprecedented in the annals of juvenile cadging, and he complimented me highly on the very able manner in which I had performed my business. That night I was indulged with an extra supper, and an allowance of grog, which I drank with a very good palate after my day's exertions, nay, so far had I already advanced in all the appendages of my new calling, that I actually attempted and succeeded in the very difficult task of smoking a pipe, after the most approved example of my young companions.

"Thus being once broken into my new profession, I pursued it with that industry and perseverance that soon obtained for me the enviable cognomen of " *Scapegrace Jack*," and I ruled with a supreme will over all the rest of my companions, being, of course an especial favourite with Mr. Bunckey. I now lost all remembrance of my former insipid course of life, and looked back with a great deal of inward pleasure to that memorable night, that by sleeping in the celebrated Mrs. Bott's *snoozing ken* I had met with Messrs. Stokes and Miles, by whose means I was indebted for my present situation and prospects in life. I continued the lucrative profession of the poor orphan boy, until I had grown out of it, and was then of course, compelled to adopt some other occupation, and figure in a new character. I had for some time past being on rather *intimate* terms with a young *lady* of our firm who figured in the character of a vender of ballads, and who possessing, in my estimation, at that time the most superlative

accomplishment of a very free and good natured disposition, had managed to secure to herself the whole honour of my particular attentions. This young lady, who had of late found an unaccountable falling off in the sale of the children of the *muse*, had been advised by Mr. Bunckey to attempt a new "*move ;*" but had hitherto rejected all the offers he had made to her, either from a praiseworthy attachment to her former profession, or a dislike to the new methods he had proposed, but at length I hit upon a scheme which not only met with her warmest concurrence, but with the approbation of Mr. Bunckey. This plan was, that Mr. Bunckey should hire a couple of 'children for Sarah Bubbit, and we should both embark in a new line of business as man and wife. But do not imagine that it was my intention to commit the crime of matrimony ; oh, no, I entertained at that time the most sovereign contempt for the church and all its rites, and was so peculiarly averse to any thing in the shape of shackles, that I was resolved at any rate, if I wore any at all, they should not be those of Cupid. The fact is, it was resolved that me and Sarah should appear in the streets as a poor distressed young man and his wife, with their two starving babes, and it will be probably deemed sufficient for me to say, that our plan succeeded quite as well as our most sanguine hopes had anticipated, until Sarah by some *mistake* happened to be accused at the *Old Bailey* of *borrowing* something in the shape of a silver watch and its appendages, by which manœuvre, she was provided with a government situation, without any trouble, for seven years, certain. I was thus once more thrown upon my own resources, but was not long in hitting upon a new character, my next performance being that of a poor wretched cripple upon crutches.

" Thus passed away several years of my eventful life, and so great had become my success, and my influence over the rest of the gang, that I began to be discontented with my present situation, and to reflect upon the means of altering it. Although I was not quite ' *green*' enough to be very correct in my accounts with Mr. Bunckey, yet I thought what

I did give him out of the fruits of my talents might as well be in my own pocket; and although I was well aware of his power over the officers, and the many tricks he had before played his refractory victims, yet I resolved at all hazards to risk his vengeance, and make a bold venture on my own account. I had scarcely formed this resolution, when Mr. Bunckey was taken very ill, and notwithstanding all the advice he had, he was compelled to give up his worldly accounts in less than a week, after very kindly leaving me a hundred pounds, for my unexampled exertions in the good cause, and free leave to go wherever I pleased with the rest of my companions, for it was Mrs. Bunckey's intention to retire from business. This was an event that afforded me the most unspeakable pleasure; I had never so much money in my possession before, and although I had come to no conclusion in my own mind as to my future plans, I pocketed the cash, bade good bye to Mrs. Bunckey, and the members of the gang, and started forth in quest of other adventures, with brighter prospects than I had hitherto enjoyed.

"I had pursued my way as far as High Street, Bloomsbury, before I had come to any exact conclusion whither I should direct my steps, or what I should be at; when suddenly a thought darted across my brain, that as I was now in the possession of money, I would try my fortune in the 'gentleman' line; and with that admirable idea, determined to lose no time, and noticing the inappropriate state of my wardrobe for the character, I turned into that celebrated emporium for renovated toggery and long nosed Jews, *Monmouth Street*!

"The lipey into whose establishment I hied myself, looking at the heterogeneous and maze-like fashion in which I was at present equipped, imagined that I wanted a suit of not much higher pretensions, it was therefore with extreme difficulty, and not until I had several times assured him of my readiness and ability to pay him for a genteel suit, that I could tempt him to bring me down any thing like a fashionable looking apparel. At length, however, after trying upon me a dozen of the largest and ugliest coats that any schneider could possibly concieve, which he solemnly protested fitted me '*like vaxsh*,' and the same quantity of trowsers of the most circumscribed dimensions, which he as firmly assured me, fitted me 'ash if dey had been made for me!' I succeeded in obtaining a very smart turn out, in which I attired myself forthwith, and having also purchased a new hat, and a pair of Wellingtons, I left the Jew my discarded clothes by way of a memento, and with a feeling of conscious pride and dignity I had never experienced before, I strutted forth into the streets in my new and taking character.

"I will not tax your patience by relating every particular of the preliminaries I made use of to establish myself as a gentleman, having received a moderate education for the short time I was at school, and possessing natural talents of no mean order, I was in every way calculated to succeed, therefore behold me established in a fashionable hotel, not a thousand miles from Bond Street, figuring away as the only son of a rich East Indian Nabob, in the good graces of the proprietor, and on the most friendly terms with all the residents at the hotel, who seemed not to entertain the slightest idea of the daring imposition I was practising upon them.

"By the most fortunate chance I became acquainted with a set of *black-legs*, who on being made acquainted with my former history, thought me worthy of becoming one of them; they therefore took great pains to initiate me into all the secrets of their art, and as I was remarkably quick at learning any thing, it was not long before I was as accomplished in the art of 'shirking or feathering a goose,' as the most experienced amongst them. We were very successful, and that enabled me to carry on with the greater success the character I was personating. Many were the unfortunate dupes whom we plundered nightly, and yet did I manage every thing with such good grace, that my conduct was never for a moment suspected by my *friends* at the hotel.

"Among the rest of the gentlemen was a young man who was the son of a wealthy baronet, who resided in one of the fashionable squares, and to whom he undertook to introduce me. The old baronet was very much pleased with me, and warmly invited me to visit him often; with this invitation I of course did not fail to comply, but it was not alone on account of the old baronet,—oh, no, I had another object in view, and one which was of such a tempting and lovely description that half the hearts of the aristocratic juvenility were in a state of actual fury to obtain a smile from it. This object was a female, and this female the beauteous and accomplished daughter of the baronet. She was scarce eighteen, was lovely in the extreme, accomplished and virtuous; and yet I had the presumption to look up to this interesting and invaluable object, with an idea of becoming possessed of her. Nay, it may not be believed, but I am ready to pledge *my veracity*,—that so far was I successful as to make myself in a very short time agreeable to the young lady, and at last so far captured her as to draw from her a candid acknowledgment of love, and a reference to her father. How far successful I might have been I cannot say, but fortune was now about to play her vagaries with me; some person had, by means with which I could never become possessed, become acquainted with the whole of my singular history and real character, and very kindly communicated the facts to the baronet, on the very morning I was going to propose myself to him as his son-in-law. I was apprised of the fact by some of my colleagues of the gaming table in time, and not thinking it politic to hazard a personal appearance either to the baronet, or at the hotel at which I had been staying, I bade good bye to fashion an hour afterwards, and mounting on the top of a Bath coach, forthwith took my departure from London.

"I was perfectly well aware that all my prospects in the line I had been lately playing were blighted for ever; but as I happened to have a good round sum by me, the proceeds of my transactions at the gaming table, I did not trouble myself with thinking of what I should do in future for the present. I lived some time a life of indolent luxury at Bath, and could have been content to have remained in the same situation for the rest of my life, but my ready cash began to look most alarmingly low, and it became indispensably necessary for me to devise some means of replenishing my purse.

"It was not long before my inventive faculties furnished me with an idea, which seemed likely to bring me plenty of *grist to the mill*. During my brief intercourse with fashionable life, I had been careful to elicit all the particulars of the family histories and connections of the persons with whom I mingled, thinking that they might at some future period be of service to me, and I now determined to turn them to account, by turning begging letter writer. In this I succeeded marvellously, sometimes representing myself as a distant relative of the parties to whom I wrote, and at other times calling myself the son of a distinguished military officer, who had lost his life in the service of his country, and left me in a condition that soon reduced me to beggary. The very pathetic manner in which I wrote all these epistles, and the apparent sincerity in which I clothed them, brought me many and valuable contributions, and I succeeded in duping among the rest, my old friend the baronet out of ten pounds, by the same means. But at length I became suspected, and the glaring prospect of a sea voyage induced me to abandon that way of living, not, however, before I had managed to scrape together a pretty good quantity of *gold dust*, which I laid by for a rainy day in the Bank of England.

"By way of a change, I now returned to my old occupation of cadging, which I prosecuted for several years in various characters with remarkable good luck, and kept adding the honey to the hive in very good style; till at last having endured a number of ups and downs and plenty of *crosses*, I determined to take to a *crossing*, which proved to be the most profitable of all my pursuits, although the way of accumulating *ochre* in that manner is certainly a dirty one. Gentlemen, I have now given you the whole of my adventures, and if they have afforded you half as much amusement in listening to the recital of them, as I have experienced in meeting with them, I am amply repaid for the trouble I have been at in detailing them, and it is my sincere wish that every respectable cadger that I now see around me, may meet with the same success that has attended the pursuits of ' *Scapegrace Jack* !'

Here this most remarkable individual sat down, amid the most tumultuous applause, having come to the conclusion of that extraordinary history, which had delighted his learned auditors for so many evenings. Some hours having been then devoted to mirth, the august members of the *Cadgers' Society* separated.

CHAP. VI.

IN WHICH IS COMMENCED ANOTHER MOST EXTRAORDINARY HISTORY—BEING THE ADVENTURES, TRICKS, ARTIFICES, AND AMOURS OF DICK THE VAGRANT, *alias* GENTLEMAN RICHARD.—SOME ACCOUNT OF THE PARENTAGE OF OUR HERO.—A PROMISING CHARACTER.—A BOLT—AND AN AMOUR IN SPAIN.

THE autobiography of " *Scapegrace Jack*," had excited the deepest interest in the minds of all who had heard it, and having been duly entered on the papers of *the Club*, was left as a lasting memento of the extraordinary career of one of the most remarkable and learned cadgers that ever existed.

The members of the club were all anxious for the next meeting, when it was currently reported, nay, universally believed, and generally whispered, that the most accomplished and amiable Jeremiah Jumper would detail the particulars of his mortal race; and, of course, every person looked forward with the most splendid anticipations to any thing that might fall from the lips of their honourable and distinguished secretary; but the next evening arrived, and the illustrious members of *the Cadger's Club*, were doomed to be most wofully disappointed; for notwithstanding that there

was a motion from the chairman, that all other members of the Club " do give precedence, in this history of their adventures, to their respected founder Jeremiah Jumper, Esquire," notwithstanding that this motion was carried without a dissentient voice, and hallooed, hammered, knocked, thumped, bawled, and squalled, with all due honours, Jeremiah Jumper in a very neat speech protested he " vould see 'em all blowed fust," for two or three very substantial reasons, which we do not think we should be exactly justified in betraying in this history; in consequence of which resolution Jeremiah Jumper sat down, and paid his very best respects to half a gallon of delightful hot, and smoked forth ten cigars in one hour to compose his feelings; and the rest of the company set themselves to work to cast lots to see upon whom the task to relate his adventures should devolve : it was soon decided; the party upon whom it fell, was a middle aged man attired in a nautical dress, and who, to judge from his appearance, must have been conceived in the ocean and cradled on board a ship. How far his career would justify these surmises will be fully detailed The announcement of the name of " *Dick, the Vagrant*," for the next autobiography, was received with the loudest acclamations, and due time having been given to allow that gentleman to collect. his thoughts, silence was obtained and in a clear and distinct voice thus launched forth into

The Life and Career of

DICK, THE VAGRANT;

ALIAS

GENTLEMEN RICHARD !!

" Unlike the honourable Jack, whose adventures have lately afforded us such infinite amusement, I was born in the house of affluence, and owe all the miseries I may have experienced, and my being reduced—(if such it can be called) to my present mode of life, to my own extravagance, folly, and dissipation. I am the only son of a gentleman, who possessed large estates in the county of Durham, and whose ancient family had for ages upheld their dignity and pride above all others of the gentry around. When I say that I was the only child of a fond indulgent mother, and an equally kind and affectionate father, it will not be considered a matter of astonishment that the greatest care should be bestowed on the cultivation of my mind, and that I should be indulged to that excess which afterwards was the cause of my future vices; all the hopes of my amiable parents were fixed on me and it was fondly anticipated by them that I should hand down their name with honour to future generations;—alas! they were most egregiously deceived!—

"I very soon gave notice of a most incorrigible, petulent, and reckless disposition, scorning the advice of my parents, and spurning alike at controul. Thus passed away the early years of my life, until I was sent to the University of Oxford, where my becoming acquainted with several young gentlemen, whose dispositions assimilated with my own, did not tend you may be certain to improve my moral understanding, or bring me to a sense of the ultimate ruin my conduct must bring upon me. My demands upon my father's purse were frequent and heavy, and although he remonstrated with me very properly on the folly of my conduct, it excited no other feeling in my callous bosom than contempt. At length, however, my dissipation was such, and my calls for remittances so frequent, that my father became completely tired of them, and sent me a severe letter, in which he expressed his firm determination no longer to yield to my extravagance, and to remit me no more than the sum he had at first set apart for my wants. This letter greatly exasperated me, and I did not hesitate to designate my amiable father a stingy old curmudgeon; but I had soon no cause to regret his parsimony; for in less than a week I received a communication from my mother, in which she affectionately exhorted me to reform my conduct, and to encourage me to obey her, sent me a large sum of money, which came in very opportunely for me to pay several considerable debts which I had contracted at the gaming table, and to quiet several amatory peccadilloes in which I had been engaged about the city. How well I adhered to my mother's advice will be shewn in the course of my narrative.

"A circumstance soon afterwards occurred, which caused me to leave Oxford in rather a hasty and unexpected manner. Having excited the jealousy of one of my fellow collegiates, by an amour with a female with whom he was on intimate terms, he was so exasperated that he challenged me to fight a duel. Naturally passionate, and not at all in want of courage, I did not refuse the invitation; we met according to appointment, and I had the misfortune to shoot my adversary dead. Having partially recovered from the horror into which I was thrown by this fatal event; I was fully sensible of the critical situation in which I was placed, and saw no other means of escaping from the most ignominious predicament, than by taking to immediate flight. By the assistance of my seconds, I therefore put this determination into instant effect, and, having procured a horse at the nearest inn, was soon tearing away, at the utmost speed, from the scene of the awful catastrophe. In the utmost state of exhaustion, and fatigued and disheartened, I reached at last the neighbourhood in which my parents resided. I did not venture to the house of my father, and it was very well I did not, for the news had arrived there before me, and officers were on the look-out for my apprehension. I hastened into an obscure tavern a few miles from my father's residence, where I was unknown, and contrived to despatch a letter, with great secrecy, to my father, apprising him of my arrival, and requesting to see him as soon as possible. The good old gentleman lost no time in coming to me, and it would be impossible for me to do adequate justice to my father's feelings on that occasion, or to the state of agony in which he described my excellent mother to be. He pointed out to me, in the mildest manner, the awkward dilemma in which my follies, or rather vices, had placed me, and in the most affectionate manner exhorted me to reform my conduct ere it might be too late to save myself from the most disgraceful consequences.

I felt the justice of his remarks, and made many promises to repent, if I could but extricate myself from my present perilous situation, which at the time I really meant to perform. There was no time to be lost; some means must be adopted to effect my escape from the country, until my friends could manage to settle the business with the relatives of the unfortunate deceased. A plan was very soon devised; the son of a gentleman of my acquaintance, who lived at some distance, was about to go on a continental tour, and to his father my parent addressed a letter, stating the particulars of my circumstances, and requesting that he would allow me to accompany his son on his journey. This etter he immediately despatched by the post, and at midnight, after a very affectionate parting with my parents, and with a well-filled purse, set off on my departure to the house of Mr. Clermont. I arrived quite safe, and Mr. Clermont, having received my father's letter, met me very kindly, and expressed his willingness to serve me all that laid in his power. Arthur Clermont, his son, and I had been old friends, and he was very well pleased to have me for a companion. The next morning, I being disguised as his domestic, we departed, and very quickly were on board the ship, which was bound for Spain. By the time we had arrived at the place

No. 11.

of our destination, my natural volatile disposition, the good humour of my companion, and the anticipation of the life and variety we should mingle in, had almost entirely effaced from my memory the fatal cause of my leaving England, and I began to consider and to consult with Arthur, the best manner in which we could pass our time agreeably. Spain was a country every way qualified to afford me the gratification my wild and adventurous disposition delighted in, and it was not very long before I had an opportunity of giving free indulgence to it.

"Arthur Clermont was young and good-looking, with a daring spirit, an inordinate love of gallantry, and with a romantic disposition, that was continually leading him into scrapes and difficulties, and in which I being at all times willing to become his most faithful ally, we were perpetually in the midst of some dilemma or the other.

"It happened that one day, when Arthur was taking a stroll through the city by himself, he caught a glimpse of a damsel at a castellated mansion, and judging, from the pensive style of her beauty, that she must necessarily be unhappy, had the egotism to fancy that he was the only identical person who was born to console her.

"Such was the impression that this fair Spanish lady made upon the susceptible and gallant Arthur, that he found it impossible to gain any rest, until by a variety of artifices with which the brains of sanguine lovers are generally very prolific, he managed to wheedle Inez, the young lady's waiting-maid, by the dint of a purse and a kiss, to persuade her fair mistress that he was ' a sweet young man,' the consequence of which persuasion was, that the damsel suffered her compassion to prevail over her prudence, and in spite of the wrath she knew she would experience, should her old lynx-eyed guardian discover it, granted him an interview; so Arthur scaled the garden-wall, and flung himself at Elvira's feet, declaring himself one of the most wretched of men, and the most constant of lovers.

"Elvira pretended to be very much astonished at his audacity, but was not at all displeased with his handsome English face, but of course she bade him quit her presence, and never presume to appear in it again. Whether from his imperfect knowledge of Spanish, he did not exactly comprehend the latter part of the injunction, or, becoming sensible afterwards of the heinousness of the the offence was anxious to evince his penitence, I know not, but it is an indubitable fact that he was in the very same spot and presence on the following day, and every day for a week after, by which time he had by some means or other, so far ingratiated himself into Elvira's favour, that she no longer objected to his visits, which were consequently very frequently repeated; be it understood, however, that they were visits of the most prudent nature, being always conducted in the presence of the faithful Inez. It was not long before Arthur elicited from Elvira every particular of her situation; she was very rich, but in the guardianship of a distant relative, who was the owner of the castello, and who was very anxious to repair with her property his own mutilated fortunes. The old hidalgo had the peculiar recomendation of one of the ugliest faces ever seen, a hump upon his shoulder, a disagreeable temper, and a beautiful asthma. The old coger had been absent for some weeks on a visit to a friend in a distant part of the country, and it was quite uncertain when he would return. Arthur, therefore felt perfectly safe in his visits, and was so bold as to venture to take me in on one occasion. The silly fellow, he little expected what a train he was thus unconsciously laying to blow up his fair citadel of hope. I was thus introduced to a pair of the most beautiful black eyes I had ever before beheld, and was graciously received by the lovely Elvira, with whom I was immediately captivated, and as I have before shewn I was not particularly nice as regarded honour, I did not hesitate a moment in forming a determination in my own mind to supplant my friend in the possession of the affections of the Spanish damsel. In this design, I must in justice to myself say, that I was strongly encouraged by the marked favour which the lady shewed towards me; and sundry little glances which were on the sly darted upon me by the before-mentioned beautiful black twinklers; therefore I resolved to let no opportunity pass of making myself more at home with Elvira.

" We had just succeeded in making ourselves particularly agreeable to Elvira on the day of the visit of which I am speaking, and were perfectly happy in one of the sweetest conversations I at that time ever experienced, which only wanted the absence of Arthur at that time to make it truly felicitous to me, when Inez, whose attention had been drawn towards the castello by some unusual bustle, came running into the apartment in great alarm, with the astounding intelligence that the hidalgo had returned and with his retinue, was at that moment approaching the room. Upon this announcement, we, of course, saw the necessity of immediate flight, unless we preferred being impaled alive on some dozen or two of Spanish rapiers, so we hastily sounded a retreat, which was made in none of the most accomplished of styles, at least on my part. Arthur mounted the ladder, which was of rope, first gained the top of the wall, and let himself down on the other side ; when I prepared to follow him; but, unfortunately, before I had ascended above half way, the confounded apparatus broke, and I was precipitated into a rose bush, out of which I scrambled with my face and hands most elegantly inlaid with thorns, and discoloured with blood.

" Many of the honourable members present," continued ' Gentleman Richard,' " may consider me tedious in thus minutely detailing all the particulars of my life previous to the events which followed in my professional career ; but I think it indispensably necessary that I should narrate them, not only on account of their being remarkably interesting and laughable, but also to shew the singular adventures which ultimately removed me from the character of a gentleman to that of a beggar."

The learned Jeremiah Jumper and his associates having expressed the infinite delight every portion of the narrative afforded them, ' Gentleman Richard'

continued his history in the following words :—

" I had no time to re-unite the ladder, for I had scarcely gathered myself up from among the mutilated roses, when the heavy tread of several footsteps sounded in my ears, and had no other alternative than to trust to the guidance of the artful Inez, (who had accompanied me and my friend to the garden to secure our flight,) who led me through an obscure covered avenue to a low door, that led into a chapel connected with the castello, where she left me with injunctions to remain quite still until her return. Inez, however, was gone such a considerable time, that fearing she had forgotten me, I was about to make a desperate attempt to escape by myself, when the door opened, and a figure enveloped in a grey mantle advanced cautiously towards me. With a caution for me to be silent, the person threw off the mantle, and I then discovered the long expected waiting-maid of Donna Elvira. In as few words as possible she gave me her reasons for appearing in such a disguise, and the use she had in view for it. It appeared according to her account, that there was a tradition of an old warrior attached to the castello, who was reported to have been murdered many years before, and who was buried beneath the very place on which we were then standing, and was reported to haunt the chapel every night wrapped up in a grey mantle. Now, it appeared, according to a portrait of the old knight which was preserved in one of the apartments of the castello, that I happened to resemble him very much; so the cunning Inez thought, and wisely too, that with the addition of the grey mantle, and the scarifications of the rose bush fresh upon my visage, I might pass in a crowd for the spirit of the chapel. The hidalgo's retainers, she also informed me, were at that moment assembled in the hall, listening to one of the old steward's horrible ghost stories, so consequently a famous opportunity was afforded me. She desired me to follow close upon her heels, and when she screamed out, I was to stalk into the hall, make my way with much ghostly dignity to the door, when I was to take to my heels with all the expedition I could, clear the gate, and beyond which the good natured little maiden informed me that I should find Arthur Clermont and a horse waiting for me.

"I should have showered upon Inez a thousand expressions of my gratitude, only time was very precious; and I therefore hastily arrayed myself in my ghostly apparel, and followed her to the entrance of the hall as she had directed me to do. No sooner had we arrived there then she rushed in, and throwing down the lamp which she had carried in her hand, screamed out most lustily, 'The spectre! the spirit! the ghost! the devil!' Away I bounded after her, the party making way for me on both sides, and tumbling over one another, in their alarm and eagerness to shield themselves from my supernatural power. One desperate fellow, however, who had not evinced the consternation of his companions, seemed very much inclined to dispute my passage; and it would have been extremely impolitic in me to risk my spiritual reputation in an encounter with him. I should have been placed in a most perilous situation, had not my guardian angel, in the shape of Inez, flown to my rescue, and, by rushing to him as if for protection, clung so closely to him that he was unable to arrest my progress. Before the rest of the retainers had recovered from their terror, I cleared the gate, and finding my friend and the horse, as Inez had informed me, waiting my arrival, in a very short time afterwards we arrived in safe quarters.

"It soon appeared, after this adventure, that the beauteous Elvira had not hastily forgotten the impression I had made upon her; in a few days afterwards I received a private communication from her, which expressed, in the most affectionate manner, her feelings towards me, and informing me that the old hidalgo was again absent from the castello—therefore, if I had any wish to see her again, she would contrive to see me—that I must go in disguise, to prevent any suspicion among the neighbours—that Inez would be waiting for me in a certain place, and in order to make myself known to her, I was to place the ring she had seen me wear, on

the serving-maid's finger, when she would immediately conduct me to her presence. As regarded Arthur Clermont, she assured me that since she had seen me, he was hateful to her; and in order that his suspicion of her regard for me might not be excited, she had taken the precaution to forward him an epistle, in which she informed him that the hidalgo kept such a vigilant eye upon her, that she knew not when she should be able to see him again, but that she would apprise him of the first opportunity that presented itself.

"I could scarcely believe the evidence of my eyes as I read this letter, but I was soon convinced of the reality of it, and also of the sincerity of what the charming Elvira had stated as regarded Arthur; for, with a very melancholy countenance, he showed me the letter, and requested my advice upon it, which I gave in such a manner as to drown his suspicions, and materially to benefit my own cause. I then informed him that I had just received a communication from my father, which would require my presence for a day or two in another part of the country, and should depart on the following day. This scheme answered as well as I could have anticipated it would, and having got rid of my friend, who seemed in no spirits for society, I set about putting my stratagem into execution, and after thinking of various disguises, which I afterwards abandoned, I at length very wisely determined to assume the dress of an ancient duenna, as one the least likely to excite curiosity. By the aid of a very cunning fellow, whom I retained in the capacity of my valet, I soon obtained the necessary dress, and the following morning, at an early hour, we both departed on our adventure. When we had arrived at a posado not far from the street where I was to meet Inez, with the landlord of which my valet was acquainted, and did not hesitate to impart to him my secret, we stopped, and were shown into a private room, where, with the assistance of my faithful valet, I was shortly attired, and by the help of a stoop, a feeble hobble, and a stick, I looked the duenna admirably. This was my first appearance in character, and I do not flatter myself when I assure you, that I acquitted myself in a manner which augured well for my future success in the art of deception, and which I have since practised with such extraordinary good fortune.

"After having followed me at a distance, to see if I might require his aid, my servant left me upon seeing me address myself to the pretty waiting-maid of Elvira, who was already at the place of appointment, and anxiously awaiting my arrival. She congratulated me in a whisper, upon the skill with which I had accomplished my disguise, and then, by a number of bye ways, led me to the castello, and quickly afterwards into the presence of that lovely being upon whom all my thoughts and wishes at that period were fixed. I will not describe the meeting, which was very speedily put to an unexpected termination.

"Twice had the divine Elvira permitted me to press her vermillion cheeks, and I was in the act of throwing myself on my knees to assure her of the ardour of my passion, when I heard my inamorato scream; and, looking up, judge of my confusion and consternation when I beheld the frightful and enraged old hidalgo standing behind me, his hideous features dreadfully distorted with passion, and his eyes flashing vengeance upon me. He had been an unobserved watcher of my actions since my first introduction to the chamber of his ward, until, unable longer to contain himself, he had rushed forth in the manner I have described.

"One of his accursed domestics, a rejected admirer of the pretty Inez, having, by some means or other only known to himself, discovered the whole plot, in a spirit of revenge he had communicated it to his master, and the hateful old hidalgo, instead of going a long journey, as he pretended, had retired to a neighbouring posado, where he had awaited impatiently the hour of my arrival, which he had no sooner heard chimed forth by a neighbouring convent bell, than he returned to his castello, and entering it by a secret passage, made his way to a small closet adjoining Donna Elvira's chamber. At first the old savage had determined to blow my brains out upon the spot; but he afterwards abandoned that idea, and resolved to inflict upon me a punishment of greater severity, and more commensurate with what he considered the *heinousness* of my crime."

"*Gentleman Dick*" stopped when he had arrived at this interesting portion of his story; and as he wanted time to collect his thoughts, and also to arrange them, he solicited permission of his *honourable* friends to resume it on the following night. With a request so reasonable, they of course could not refuse to comply, and the drinkables were accordingly sent merrily about, for the purpose of finishing up the night.

"Dick's" narrative was of that romantic nature, that it completely enchained the attention of his listeners, and they unanimously agreed that, for deep interest, originality, and variety, it was every way worthy of being placed in competition with the "*Autobiography of 'Scapegrace Jack.*'" In fact, many of the learned cadgers declared, that it by far surpassed the recital of that clever gentleman, inasmuch as the greater portion of what he had related was of a sombre caste, and not exactly suited to the taste, of many of the members who had listened to it.

Pleased with the numerous but certainly well merited compliments that were so flatteringly bestowed upon him, "*Gentleman Dick*" set his memory and his ingenuity to work, and by the following evening he had linked such a chain of incidents together, which certainly if they did not augur much in favour of his veracity, shewed the prolific powers of his invention, and are quite sufficient for the purposes for which they are intended; namely, amusement, and, it is hoped, instruction.

CHAP. VII.

THE REMARKABLE ADVENTURES OF "DICK, THE VAGRANT," CONTINUED.—A DUCK IN THE QUADIL-QUIVER, AND A DUCK IN A COTTAGE. — THE STRATAGEM, AND THE FLIGHT FROM SPAIN.

"UNFORTUNATELY for myself," resumed '*Gentleman Richard*,' on the following evening, " I had brought nothing with me to defend myself in case of surprise, in fact, I had never once anticipated such an occurrence, where as the infernal hidalgo was armed from head to heel, and by way of commencement, he flourished a Spanish rapier over my head, as long as a moderate roasting spit; Elvira had fainted, and I was supporting her in my arms, when the heap of deformity which composed the carcase of the antiquated hidalgo, advanced furiously towards me, and attempting to snatch the insensible beauty from my arms, demanded in as loud a voice as his lungs would allow him to display, what villain I was.

"To this question I did not condescend to reply, only by a frown, but I retained my hold of Elvira, and was looking around the room for an ottoman on which to deposit her inanimate form, being determined at all hazards to make an attack upon the hidalgo, in spite of his long rapier, and not doubting but from my youth, strength, and agility, I should be able to vanquish him; but I had reckoned without my host upon that occasion, for the old Spaniard, doubtless imagining my intentions, was determined to thwart me, and stamping loudly on the floor of the apartment with his foot, the next moment the door flew open, and about a dozen stout fellows all well armed, rushed in, and quickly surrounded me.

"Resistance would now have been worse than madness, so I was compelled to submit passively to my fate, which I expected would be a severe one. The old hidalgo having consigned my inamorato to the care of the women, I was borne into another apartment, and being stripped to the waist by the orders of my ferocious enemy, one of the stoutest of the fellows was deputed to give me a sound flogging, and which I must do him the justice to say, he did with much skill, to the evident satisfaction of his master, who watched my writhings on the pillar to which I was bound, with infinite gratification. I need not attempt to describe to you the state of my feelings on this occasion, I could have shot the whole of the scoundrels for the ignominy they were daring to inflict upon me; but it was fruitless for me to complain, I being in their power, and complaints being only calculated to exasperate them the more against me. To continue however.

"After I had received at least, I am certain, one hundred and fifty lashes from a sword sheath, I was unfastened from the whipping post or pillar, dressed, and my hands being bound together, a consultation was held between the hidalgo and his domestics as to the most advisable manner in which they could dispose of me. One proposed cutting my throat; another suggested the propriety of blowing my brains out, a third prescribed imprisonment beneath the castello, and a fourth was for having me hanged in the gardens, to the highest tree they could find; however the old hidalgo was kind enough to reject all these *merciful* propositions, but came to a determination to run the hazard of breaking my neck, he having ordered them to tie me hand and foot, and toss me out of the casement of the north tower of the castello. I protested most loudly against this remorseless decree, and threatened the old hidalgo with the severest punishment, if he put his barbarous threat into execution, but he only grinned triumphantly in my face, and desired his fellows to do as he had commanded them. In vain I kicked,—in vain I struggled,—in vain I called for mercy, threatened, and swore by turns, my hands and feet were bound together by the merciless myrmidons of the old and savage hidalgo, and before I could utter a single exclamation, I was carried into the north tower, and thrown from a first floor casement, amid the laughter of the ferocious minions, and the savage exultation of Elvira's guardian.

"Fortune, however, happened to be in one of her most favorable moods, and saved my neck at the hazard of the neck of a passenger beneath. It occured most providentially for me, that at the very moment I was thrown from the casement, an old woman happened to be passing beneath, with a basket of eggs upon her head, into which I fell plump, smashing all the eggs, capsizing the old woman, and rolling with her cheek by jowl into the kennel. The old woman not having met with any serious personal injury. arose from the kennel with much fury and seeing the damage I had done to her goods, she commenced a most diabolical attack upon my person, which being bound hand and foot, as I have before stated, I was, of course, unable to resist, and in which a number of idle fellows, who had witnessed the whole adventure, and enjoyed the fun vastly, joined her, and I stood every chance of meeting with much severer punishment than that I had previously encountered in the hidalgo's castello, had I not vociferated most lustily for quarter, and my assailants having nearly exhausted themselves by the violence of the attack they had made upon me, desisted for a moment, and inquired who I was. I showed them the manner in which I was pinioned, and endeavoured to explain the meaning of it; but no sooner did they behold the condition I was in, then they one and all declared I was a thief, and a loud cry was raised for them to bear me to prison before the *Corregidor*, and in spite of my expostulations, I was quickly raised in the arms of two or three stout fellows, and borne to prison immediately; the old woman following to get indemnification for her broken eggs.

"After having been kept in custody for about two or three hours, to await the appearance of the *Corregidor*, I was brought before him, and having invented a plausible story to account for the singular situation in which I had apparently dropped from the clouds, I was discharged upon condition of paying the old woman for her eggs. With this sentence, I very readily complied, and being unbound, and having discarded all the remnants of my late disguise, with a sore back, a sore heart, and with a most disturbed mind, I made my way immediately to the posado, in which I had expected to find my valet waiting for me; but he having stayed there, until he was exhausted, and forming an idea, that in all probability, I intended to remain where I was all night, he had returned home. As my face was pretty well cemented together with the yolks of the poor old woman's eggs that I had

smashed, and my dress was very much disordered, owing to the rough treatment I had received, the worthy host offered me every accommodation to renovate my appearance and comfort; which task having accomplished, I sat down to drink a bottle of wine, and to endeavour to compose my feelings after the rough treatment I had received, My reflections, you may rest assured, were none of the pleasantest description. I had been interrupted in one of the most delicious interviews with my inamerated, whom it was more than probable, I should never behold again, as the hateful old hidalgo would doubtless remove her to some part of the country, where there was no chance of my ever encountering her again;—I had also been degraded, and my bosom was burning for vengeance without any prospect of my ever being able to gratify it.

"It was quite dark when I left the posado, and directed my footsteps towards my home, but I had not proceeded far when the moon burst forth with all that majesty and grandeur, and peculiar brightness with which she is ever seen in an Italian or a Spanish sky. Spain is a nation of intrigue and adventure, and it was not long ere I was doomed to meet with another incident, not at all beneath the ones I had so lately encountered. As I was about to turn the corner of a street, my curiosity was excited by beholding a smart handsome cavalier, wrapped in a large mantle who was conversing to a young damsel, who had the appearance of a servant. They were standing before a large building, which I recollected to have heard reported as the residence, or rather the prison of a certain lovely young lady named Almira, who, like my lover, was under the vigilant eye of a disagreeable old guardian.

My curiosity was excited, and as I had taken the precaution to place myself behind a large stone pillar, which stood conveniently on the spot, I could overhear without being seen, all that passed between them; it was not long ere I elicited sufficient to learn that it was an assignation with Almira and the cavalier, they were conversing upon, and I also found that his name was Don Geronimo.

"'If you will return in an hour,' observed the girl to whom he was speaking, 'and placing yourself under the window, and imitate the mollrowing of a cat, the old Don will by that time have retired to rest, and I will admit you to Almira's presence!'

"'Bless you! bless you, for this, my sweet Antoniette,' replied the cavalier, pressing something into the girl's hand, 'I will not fail to come, and to do as you have desired me!'

"With these words Don Geronimo flew out of sight, and Antoniette, entered the mansion. I have before convinced you, that I am not altogether nice upon those points, which people generally call honour, and consider my own enjoyment paramount to every thing else; you will not therefore be astonished when I inform you, that the idea of this intrigue pleased me vastly, and I felt anxious to have a sight of the lovely Almira; I therefore at all hazards resolved to be there instead of Don Geronimo, and make sure of my getting into the presence of Almira, by being there at least ten minutes before him. What all tended to assist my resemblance to the cavalier, about whose height and figure I was, enveloped in a mantle of the same make and colour as the one he wore, and which I had left at the posado previous to assuming my disguise, but which I had of course resumed upon returning to the inn.

"In order that I might be certain that Geronimo had not arrived before me, I did not leave my present place of concealment, but looking at my watch to observe the time, I awaited anxiously the moment of the appointment. When it wanted about ten minutes to the time at which the cavalier had promised to be there, and I observed an unusual stillness in the house, I wrapped my mantle closely around my person, and concealing my features as much as possible, took my station under the casement, as Antoinette had directed, and commenced mollrowing in a style that would have done infinite credit to the most experienced tile travelling Tom Tabby in the universe, which was the more surprising,

as it was an accomplishment I had never before given myself credit for."

Here "*Gentleman Richard*" paused to allow his attentive auditors to indulge in a boisterous fit of laughter, which, after the lapse of several minutes, having subsided, he resumed his interesting story as follows :

"Not a second had I continued my mollrowing concerto, when the the casement immediately above my head was thrown open, and I had scarce time to retreat to my place of ambush, behind the pillar I have mentioned, when I observed an old gentleman's head pop out, ensconced in a night-cap, and from which I judged it to be the guardian of Almira, and that he had retired to repose :

"'Curse the cats!' I heard the old hunks exclaim, 'what a devil of a noise they do always make; I wish to the Saints, they would keep to their usual places of assignation, on the roofs of the houses, and not come here at this hour to disturb honest and sober people after they have just got into a comfortable nap! Oh, they seem to be all gone now, so I'll e'en retire to bed again.' And with those words, the old don made his exit from the casement, and all was quiet again. I was now, however, fearful to resume my performance for a few minutes, fearing that I might again disturb the old man; which was a very provoking thing to me, as every moment to me was precious, and I was fearful that Geronimo would arrive, and thwart all my plans. However, the rain began to descend, and I was in hopes that that would either prevent the cavalier coming altogether, or detain him sufficiently long, as to give me time to prosecute my intentions. I therefore once more ventured from my concealment, and once more began mollrowing with uncommon fidelity. In this instance I was more successful than I had been before; the old don's casement did not open; so I ventured to mollrow a little longer, and the next moment was pleased to find that it had the desired effect; the door opened slowly, and I perceived the person of Antoinette, who beckoned me towards her.

I hastened to her, and cautioning me to be silent, an injunction which I had no wish to disobey, she drew me into the hall, and closed the door silently after her. I had drawn my mantle close up into my face, so that it was impossible for any one to recognise my features, and Antoinette now made a sign for me to remove my boots, which I did, trembling all the time at the delay caused by these preliminaries; and it was not without very good reason, for I had only just began to follow Antoinette up stairs, when a loud mollrowing from without, convinced me that Geronimo had arrived. Antoinette paused in apparent surprise, and pointed significantly towards the street door, as much as to ask me what I imagined could be the reason of the noise: at that moment an idea darted across my mind, and I whispered to Antoinette, that the noise must proceed from some wicked boys whom I had observed outside, and who were thus mimicking the mollrowing I had made. This artifice succeeded. Antoinette appeared satisfied, and poor Don Geronimo was doomed to stand mollrowing out in the pelting rain, while I was being conducted to his mistress's chamber. I need not describe to you the state of suspence and anxiety to which I was reduced while I was following the footsteps of Antoinette, and during which I was reflecting on the probability or improbability of the success of my stratagem. But I had not much time for cogitation, for the next moment we stopped at the door of the apartment belonging to Donna Almira, and the next instant I found myself in the presence of one of the loveliest maidens I had ever before clapt my eyes on; Elvira, even to her appeared as nothing. No sooner had I entered, and the door closed, than the captivating Almira rushed to embrace me with the utmost freedom and affection, exclaiming :—

" ' Oh, my Geronimo ; have we than again once more met ?'

" But suddenly she started back, a livid hue o'erspread her features, and she would have fallen back had it not been for the aid of Antoinette, who flew to support her, and likewise to restrain the shriek, she would otherwise have given utterance to, for my cloak had dropped off, and the light falling strong upon my countenance, had revealed my features before she could throw her ivory arms around my neck.

" ' Blessed Virgin !' she ejaculated, ' I am betrayed ; it is not Geronimo !'

" ' Do not think so meanly of me, fair lady ;' I replied, falling with much gallantry on my knee : ' from me I assure you you need fear no harm !'

" ' Who are you ? and what brings you here ?' returned Almira, her terrors apparently swelling into haughty dignity, and conscious offended pride ;— ' for what purpose can you have availed yourself of the scheme which was meant for another, to insult the privacy of a stranger ?'

" I must acknowledge I felt not a little staggered by the dignity of Almira's manner, and for a minute or two was too much confused to reply ; but at length, recollecting the peculiarity of my situation, and the necessity for some immediate explanation on my part ; I continued on my knees, and firmly replied :—

" ' My dearest madam, I do own that my singular intrusion at this hour into your presence, and the clandestine manner by which I have effected that design

need explanation and apology from me. 'Tis true, beauteous Almira, that until the present evening you have never beheld me, although your invaluable accomplishments, and personal loveliness have been no strangers to me. Chance has entirely thrown me into your presence, and I cannot so soon consent to resign that felicity, until you have heard me plead my cause.' I then proceeded to explain the manner in which I had become acquainted with her secret, and after a long rigmarole of protestations and flattering compliments, with the recital of which I will not trouble ye, I threw myself upon her mercy. During the time I was giving this explanation, the lovely eyes of Almira were bent upon me with the mingled expressions of scorn and hatred, but by the time I had come to the conclusion of my speech, she became more composed in her manner, and did not dart upon me the rays of her anger. When I had ceased speaking, she paused, and observed me attentively for a few moments, after which she drew Antoinette aside, and held her in secret conference. When this had lasted a few minutes, she turned once more towards me, and with a look and tone of the most irresistible sweetness, she said :—

" ' You say, senor, that you are an Englishman, and consequently, if you possess the qualities of heart of the generality of your countrymen, I am confident that you will not seek to do any thing that may bring an unhappy woman to the most dreadful fate. I can allow for the strength of your feelings, and I am even ready to pardon you for the unwarrantable liberty you have taken in intruding upon my presence, on one condition only.'

" ' Name it, beauteous Almira ?' I exclaimed.

" ' Leave me directly,' she replied with much impressiveness in her manner, ' and promise me faithfully never to betray to any person what has happened this evening ?'

" ' But will you not suffer me again to behold you, fair lady ?' I ejaculated.

" ' Why do you ask it ?' replied Almira, ' when prudence and my love to Geronimo refuse it ?'

" 'But grant me another interview?' I ejaculated, 'and I swear that all that becomes a man of honour shall not be swerved from by me!'

" Almira hesitated, and again held a secret consultation with her waiting-maid, then once more turning towards me she said, offering me at the same time her delicate hand to kiss :—

" 'On the condition, senor, that you quit this place immediately, I do promise.'

" 'But when?'

" 'To morrow evening!' replied Almira, with a modest blush.

" 'At the same hour, and in the same manner?' I hastily asked. The lady nodded an assent.

" 'On that promise, lady then,' I exclaimed, 'I pledge my honour to obey you!'—Almira smiled sweetly as I said this, and bidding me adieu, I arose from my knees, and proceeded to follow Antoinette, from the room and down the stairs, in the same cautious manner in which we had entered, not a little pleased with the unexpected result of my strange adventure. When we had reached the door, I paused a moment to listen whether I could hear the mollrowing display of Don Geronimo, but all being silent, I thought myself perfectly safe, and pressing a purse into the hand of Antoinette, in order that I might secure her future good graces and assistance, the door was opened cautiously for me, and I issued into the street. I had only just gained the top of the street, and before I had recovered from the effects of my interview with Donna Almira, I heard a voice exclaim :—

" 'That's the villain, seize him!'

" The next moment I found myself roughly seized by half a dozen stout fellows, by whom I was immediately bound and gagged, and borne with rapid strides towards the noble Quadilquiver.

" Before I could make any resistance, I was thrust into a sack by the myrmidons of the jealous rival of Don Geronimo, who had mistaken me for him, and was tossed into the Quadilquiver, where my career would soon have been ended, had it not been for a worthy fisherman and his son, who were in a boat near the spot, and succeeded in hauling me up. I was borne to their cottage, and soon restored; I therefore resolved to stay there till daylight. In the morning, on entering the parlour of the cottage, judge my astonishment at beholding Elvira. The old cottager's wife, who was bed-ridden, was an object of her charity, and she called every day to see and relieve her. I need not describe our meeting; suffice it to say, that before we parted, Elvira had promised to risk every thing for me, and that we had arranged every thing for her flight from the castello, at night. We then parted, and I hastened to Arthur to excuse my absence, and to inform him that I was going to England directly. He would have persuaded me off it, for my father had been unable to come to any arrangement with the friends of the man I had slain in the duel; but of course I paid no attention to him. At night I assumed the disguise of a Spanish cavalier, and our plot succeeded; in a short time I led my Elvira from the castello to the fisherman's boat, and we were soon on board a vessel that was bound for England. A cursed fate seemed now to attend me, for just before we had reached the place of our destination, a storm arose, the ship was wrecked, and only me and four of the crew were saved; as for my Elvira, she was almost one of the first that perished. I reached England; again an infernal spell seemed to follow me: upon arriving at the place of my nativity, what was my horror to find the mansion of my parents a heap of blazing ruins, and that they had both perished in the flames. To add to my sorrow, I learned that there was a fresh claimant to the property of my father, whose right was indisputable; and thus was I deprived of every friend, and brought at once to beggary. The friends of the man I had slain, also, soon learned that I was in England, and I was forced to fly, and assume a disguise. Knowing a sweep who resided in a village a short distance off, a strange idea seized me; I bargained with him for a sooty suit of clothes, and, making my face of a suitable colour, I started on my journey. My money was all gone, and I knew not what to do. At night—tired and exhausted—I crept into an old out-house by the road side, and, crawling into a kind of loft, endeavoured to go to sleep. I had not been long there, when I heard the door open, and, looking below, saw two men enter, carrying a sack and a lantern. From their words I soon discovered that they were thieves, and that the sack contained great property, which they had just plundered. I now determined on a bold venture; so, jumping suddenly down from the loft, I stood before the thieves, who, no doubt thinking I was the devil, scampered away in great terror, and left all the property behind them. I soon removed all the portable part of the property, and by daylight found myself far on the road to London. At night I reached a low public-house, where I thought of resting; and, going into the place, the first sounds that met my ears was the most boisterous mirth and singing, from a number of voices. On entering a dark and smoky room, I beheld as motley a set of jolly beggars as ever excited the charity of the public, all drinking, smoking, dancing, eating, and generally carousing in the most jovial manner. Judging from my appearance that I was one of their craft, they invited me warmly to partake of their cheer, in which, to drown all suspicion of my real character, I coincided; although, I must confess, it was not without some fears for the safety of the money and property I had about me.

"I made up such a plausible and curious tale of my adventures, that it amused them vastly, and they highly applauded me as being an honour to the profession. The drink now again went freely round, but I—being on my guard —only pretended to drink, lest I might be overcome by the strength of the potations, and robbed of all I had about me.

"At length, one by one, the fellows became exhausted with the quantity of spirits they had drank, and dropped insensible upon the floor; and when I heard them all snoring as loud as so many pigs, I determined to make a bold effort to put my scheme into execution. I first passed the light across their eyes several times, to be certain they were really asleep, and finding that they were not pretending slumber, I proceeded, with a stout heart, to execute my design. One by one, of the unconscious wretches, did I plunder, turning their pockets inside out, and securing the contents, which altogether amounted to a good round sum. I then took the key of the door from the pocket of the apparent leader of the gang, and soon found myself once more at liberty and in the open air, having left the house without even the knowledge of the landlord.

"I had by this time amassed a good sum of money, and, being tired of the country, determined to put my former scheme into execution. I soon arrived in London, where I disposed of my booty to a Jew fence in Saffron-hill. I now re-assumed my natural apparel and complexion, and for some time led a gay life on the produce of my cunning stratagem; but that being exhausted, my taste for disguise and trickery led me once more to try the begging profession, which, I must say, I have ever found both a merry and a lucrative one."

Thus "Gentleman Richard" finished his remarkable tale, and received the loud applause of the learned members of "The Cadgers' Society."

FINIS.